BOOKS BY TIM MCBAIN & L.T. VARGUS
Casting Shadows Everywhere
The Awake in the Dark series
The Scattered and the Dead series
The Clowns
The Violet Darger series

The Scattered and the Dead

THE
SCATTERED
AND THE
DEAD

BOOK 1.5

TIM MCBAIN & L.T. VARGUS

The Scattered and the Dead

Postcards from an Empty World
Volume II

Looking back on the times just before and after the fall of civilization, I find myself fixating on people's dreams. Not the places they go during slumber, though I suppose those may be interesting enough. I'm talking about dreams in terms of their deepest hopes and desires. The visions of a better world that exist somewhere in the subconscious minds of all men and women; the unspoken state of perfection they move toward; the ideal future that shapes their view of themselves and their worlds.

These dreams, I find, were not so quick to change in the face of the death of most everyone and everything we knew. Just after, people still dreamed about types of success and pleasure that no longer existed. So often their first thought was to turn to a product for a solution to a problem, to check their phone or their email, to try to buy some comfort or shelter from pain. For a time, we still saw things through the prisms of commodities and information.

But I think during that first winter, the dreams began to adjust. And as I dug through letters and journal entries, I found more and more things buried in these dreams that disturbed me.

Four of the people we meet in this volume were documenting their time as they moved into that first winter, and one story is from before. All of them, I suppose, are confronting the deaths of the old dreams and the births of new ones.

-Baghead

3

Fiona

Beckley, West Virginia
123 days after

Winter elbowed its way inside today, the cold creeping
through the windows and floors to lay its hands on me, to
make itself felt. A nasty guest.

I built a fire in the wood stove, piling up logs and
watching them burn down to flakes of black. Orange coals
glowed within, and the iron stove went from cold to warm to
hot, kicking out intense heat that filled the room. Standing
too close made the flesh on my face feel like it was about to
bubble up into blisters.

It warmed me, perhaps, but it brought me little comfort.
How will I gather enough wood to fight this cold off every day
for months? How will I gather any wood once the snow
blankets the ground, grabbing my ankles with every step I
take?

If my count of the days is right, it would be Thanksgiving
in five days. I should be thankful to still be here when almost
no one else made it. I should be thankful for life now that it's
scarcer than ever, shouldn't I? I don't know if I am.

I try to make sense of it all. Could all of this death be part
of God's plan? Or has he left this place? Left the few of us
here? These are the end times, aren't they? If God has left us,
who does that leave in charge?

I don't know. I try to stay positive, but the days go black

faster and faster.

Doyle came by this afternoon. He brought a bunch of wood, too, hauling bundles of it in a pair of large wagons. Hard work, I suspect, for a man in his 50's. (He's only ten or so years older than me, but it somehow seems like more.)

His timing on these things remains curious to me, arriving not 45 minutes after I wrote that journal entry about needing firewood. Sometimes it's as though he can read my thoughts. As if he's trying to stave off all of my fears and worries.

And despite his kindness, I find something ghoulish about the man. Something ghastly. He smiles so much. Too much. Flashing those pointy gerbil teeth at all times, his eyes gone wide. It's a bit odd to smile like that, I think, to go around cheery like that. Everyone else is dead just about, and Doyle seems as pleased as can be to check in on me and do chores for me. Something about it makes my skin crawl.

Of course I'm not attracted to the last man on Earth, or this part of the Earth, at least. He has a bulbous forehead, perpetually shiny, and that horseshoe shaped receding hairline thing going on above it with a poof of silver hair in the center. A tuft. He has those wet, dog eyes, too. Like a sad hound of some kind. Oh, and I think I already mentioned the gerbil teeth.

Yeah.

He loaded the wood in here, pretty much doubling the stack I keep in the back room. After that, I felt bad, so I offered to make some tea. He accepted, of course.

"Getting cold now," he said.

"Yep."

Steam roiled off of the top of my tea cup, and I held it close to my nose to warm it. The inside of my nostrils felt all wet after a second, but that wasn't so bad compared to the cold. My nose is always the last part of me to get warm. It stays frigid even after the fire gets roaring to the point that I take off my jacket.

"I do enjoy a hot beverage," he said out of nowhere, sipping at his tea.

"Me too."

It felt like talking to the dental hygienist, always spouting mundane observations while they root around in your mouth with those hooks. I decided to play it like I do in that situation and not respond. He took another slug of tea and went on.

"Still cars going past on the highway. Not a lot but some. Maybe 15 or 20 a day, I guess. Isn't that crazy? That there are still people out there? Sometimes I think about going out to flag one down. Anyone. Just to talk to someone, I guess. But it's too risky. After all that's happened around here, I mean. We're better off to keep to ourselves, I expect."

I nodded, a single bob of the head. I sort of regretted acknowledging his speech. But maybe I'm too hard on Doyle. Maybe he's not so bad.

"I won't keep you," he said, tipping his head back to polish off the tea.

He looked at me with those sad dog eyes, and the guilt crept over me.

"Thanks for the wood," I said.

Lame, I know, but I didn't know what else to say. I guess even when I feel bad about it, I don't actually want to be around him.

I don't know why I keep this journal. I lost the first two notebooks worth of stuff in the move, and it didn't bother me. I didn't even look very hard. It's not like I care to look back on these horrors I've witnessed and lived.

It's not preserving these moments for future reflection that concerns me, I guess. It's the writing itself. The catharsis of recording these images and feelings that flicker over me. Somehow writing it all down expels them, purges them. The idea of sharing them makes it feel like I'm not doing this alone. It keeps me sane, at least a little. I hope so, anyway.

When you write things down, it always feels like someone is listening, doesn't it? But then I think again about that idea of God being gone, and a shiver runs down my spine. If He isn't listening anymore, who is?

Lorraine

The Compound
108 days after

Ray,

Today will be our first day apart in nine days, so I wanted to write you a quick note to put with your lunch.

You already know, of course, that the work we are doing is building something special, something bigger than either of us. If the price to be paid for that is a little time apart, so be it.

I know you'll be careful out there, and I know you'll bring more people back to our flock. Still, is it wrong that I can't wait until it snows so you have to stay home with me?

-Lorraine

Ray

Rural Maryland
108 days after

Lorraine,

I just read your note, and I am eating the sandwich you made as I write this. Have I mentioned that I hate the days when we are apart? Not to mention that I never seem to find anyone on these solo days. When you're with me, we always happen upon at least one person, you know? You must be good luck.

I do like driving, though. I guess I always did, though this is nothing like back home. The feel of the curves and dips on these mountain roads is something else entirely. Gives me that tingle in my belly. Something like riding a roller coaster, I guess. Maybe that will fade in time, but it hasn't lost its novelty yet.

These roads chiseled into the mountains are a sight to behold; the stone walls sheared off at rigid angles, strips of tar etched into the rock. I know you've seen a bit of this yourself, but every day I see new pieces of it. New mountain views. Makes me feel small somehow.

Something so striking and strange about these highways gone lifeless. Vacant aside from me and my SUV. The feeling is heightened when I'm out here on my own, and I never get used to it.

Alas, but my sandwich is gone. I'd best press on. Once I

cross a couple more towns off my list, I can get home. I can't wait. I miss you terribly.

It occurs to some part of me to shroud these feelings, to conceal them. But I am old now. I have no reason to hide anything. The truth is that it hurts me when we are apart. The loneliness twists up my guts until I'm sick with it. Maybe that's the most romantic thing a man can say to a woman – I love you so much it nauseates me.

-Ray

Fiona

Beckley, West Virginia
125 days after

I nailed moving blankets over most of the windows today. I left the living room windows just to have a room with a little light, but I did blanket up the sliding glass door in there.

Orange coals glowed in the stove while I pounded nails into the wood trim around the glass. Just enough to fight off the cold for now. The work kept me warm, too.

Strange, though, to walk through the gloom in here, shadows shrouding everything in little clouds of black that thicken into a wall as I move away from the living room. Like living in a cave or something.

I read back through yesterday's entry just now. I really need to try to be nicer to Doyle. Maybe our personalities don't mesh, but the man means well. I believe that. He has helped me so much with food and wood, let alone being a little company now and then.

I try to think about what might happen to us, Doyle and me. It's hard to look ahead. When you've seen so much death and disease and murder, it's hard to believe that a tomorrow will really come, let alone a bunch of tomorrows that stretch out into years and years. But I've been thinking about it this afternoon.

Somewhere out there, there must be groups forming. Groups of good people banding together to defend themselves from the raiders. I think Doyle and I will find one of these groups. We may need to get through the winter first, but we will find them.

That's the hope that will keep me going, I think. No matter how cold it gets.

I pulled my mattress out so I can sleep by the stove, throw in more logs during the night if I need to.

The noise comforts me. I like it when it burns real low. When the fire's breath ceases hissing, and the hot embers shimmer and crack periodically. I mean, I like to hear it roaring, too, to stare into the flicker of the flames trying to climb up the chimney chute. There's a primal joy in that, something that dates back to cavemen, I think.

Still, when it burns low and the heat still radiates off of the stove. I like that. Knowing that I'm saving a little wood, letting that residual heat wash over me for a time without burning up my resources. It warms me in a different way.

My grandma used to tell me that the antichrist would have his day. He would rise up to lead mankind to slaughter, and he would rule over the rotting remains of the Earth once most everyone was gone. Could that be what I'm living now? And if so, does that mean the antichrist is the one listening when I write here in my journal?

Fiona

Beckley, West Virginia
126 days after

I wanted to feel in control. That was all. It didn't mean anything.

Doyle sleeps now on the mattress next to the wood stove. That deep, drunken sleep that grabs someone and holds them under for a good eight or ten hours before it lets go.

We had sex tonight. (We "boinked" I think he called it at some point. Gross.)

It started with the whiskey. He brought over a few bottles just as the sun faded out of view, said it'd keep me warm, help me pass the time if I got snowed in for a day or two anytime soon.

One of them was Jim Beam black label, the kind Warner used to drink. Before all of this.

Doyle just stood in the doorway, gray light framing him. He held the four bottles out, two per hand.

"Well, I better get to heading back," he said. "It's almost dark, and it smells like snow out here already. I just wanted to check on you, really, and like I said, I thought you might enjoy these bottles if the weather turns to shit."

Part of me regretted the words I replied with before they were all the way out:

"You should stay for a drink."

I'm trying to be nicer, I guess. I don't know why I'm

13

always so cold to the man, even if he is the kind of guy to say "boink."

Anyway, his wet dog eyes blinked a few times. He had a look on his face like he'd just gotten the wind knocked out of him, and then he stepped through the door. He took off his puffy coat and lay it on the couch, sat down next to it.

I took the bottles out to the kitchen and put them on the counter.

"What will you be having?" I said, raising my voice so he'd hear me in the next room. "Whiskey or whiskey?"

He laughed.

"Oh, I'm not picky."

I poured two high ball glasses and walked back.

"No ice," I said as I handed him his drink.

"That's okay. I stored these in the garage, so they should be chilled well enough."

I drank. He was right. The cold filled my mouth, and that medicinal burn tingled all the way down. It smelled so familiar, this fermented fluid. It smelled just like Warner.

Doyle started talking then, his lips all juicy with whiskey, almost as wet as his eyes.

"Weird that it'll be Christmas before long, isn't it? I mean, sort of. With no one around – no kids and all -- I guess it won't really feel like it, but technically, you know?"

I chugged the rest of my drink.

"I'm going back for more. You want another?"

He nodded, downed the rest of his in one gulp and handed his glass over. I brought the bottle back with me. I figured we might drink more, but I liked looking at it, too, like looking at a memory.

"Do you think there are groups of people out there? Good people. There have to be right?" I said.

"I guess that must be true. The trouble is finding them, I suppose, without getting our damn heads blown off."

We got quiet for a beat, and then he licked his lips and went on.

"We'll find them, though. We might need to get through this winter first, hunker down and survive the cold, but we'll find them."

"What do you think it'll be like?"

He took a drink, held it in his mouth for a moment and then swallowed. When he talked his eyes looked far away.

"Well, I think we'll go South of here, to a place where there's no snow for years at a time. A place where the sun shines even in the winter, and the peaches are so thick they make the branches sag like slouched shoulders on all of the trees. There'll be a little colony of people. Maybe a few dozen. Maybe more. And while a bunch of us will work at harvesting the fruit and vegetables and grain, I think there'll be a group of men and women working on finding or building a working generator. A bunch of generators, really. Enough to power every home in the colony. And I think wherever you go, you'll hear the children running around to play tag and hide-and-go-seek, laughing and squealing."

He took another drink.

"That's what I think. Something like that, anyhow."

The whiskey seemed to take hold as he spoke. I felt it in my head first, like a tingling on my scalp and a dulling of my worries. Then my tongue and throat went numb with periodic needle stab feelings to accentuate the lack of sensation the rest of the time. My eyelids got heavy, too, but I didn't feel tired. Not at all.

He stood.

"I should probably get going, though. It's dark now and all."

He slid his arms into the sleeves of his green army coat and zipped it up. The truth is that I wanted him to stay, but I didn't know how to say it.

We walked to the door.

"It was nice to spend a little time together," he said. "I know I rub people the wrong way sometimes. That's just how it goes. And I know you've been through quite a lot, so I'm fine giving you plenty of space. If I'm ever encroaching on that, just let me know. I don't always have the best social awareness, but I try to."

I didn't know what to say.

"No, it's OK, Doyle. It's not like that. It's-"

He opened the door, and wisps of snow fluttered in to interrupt my scattered thought. The white blanketed everything, the light puffy stuff that piles up real high real fast. More of it spilled down out there so thick that you couldn't see more than two doors down.

Looking out that doorway with that slight buzz, it felt like the two of us were living in a snow globe that someone just gave a good shake.

"You can't walk home in this mess."

"Are you inviting me to stay?"

"I am."

Lorraine

The Compound
109 days after

Ray,

Progress continues with the repairs to the cabins. Louis reports that we have the flashing around three more leaky chimneys re-caulked. Vacancies that are all ready to be filled by the people you find out there today.

I know you still have qualms about asserting a leadership role like this. You haven't expressed it in so many words, but I know that you are concerned it will change you like it did before. That kind of power. The way it corrupts people. I get that.

But the truth is that you were born for this role. You were born to lead men, to rally people together. When you were young, you used your talents the wrong way, but you've seen enough. The doubts you express only scream all the louder that you are the man to lead this community.

-Lorraine

Ray

Outside of Alexandria, Virginia
109 days after

Lorraine,

Alexandria is a waking nightmare. The worst I've seen.
The dead walk the streets, just like all those rumors about
Florida said they did. I know we've seen a handful here and
there along the way – like the lanky one stuck in the dumpster
in Arkansas -- but this is different.

The city teems with them. They're everywhere. Stick men
and women that stumble around like drunks, shoulder to
shoulder, arms as limp as spaghetti noodles at their sides. The
skin around all of their mouths seems to peel back to expose
the teeth, lips now blackened wads of flesh bunched up along
their chins and noses. It looks like rumpled fabric crossed
with those black flaps around a dog's mouth.

They mill around in droves on the sidewalk in certain
spots, like people waiting in line to get into some venue. What
movie or concert would the dead want to attend?

They only seem vaguely interested in my passing car.
Heads wheel around in slow motion. Shoulders square toward
me in unison. The body language conveys more of a mild
curiosity than anything urgent. Perhaps they know they can't
get to me, can't outrun a car. Or maybe their understanding is
more primitive, just some sense that this sound and
movement is not food. It's difficult to say.

I drove around for quite a while just watching them. And, though it makes little sense to me, I couldn't help but find individual quirks of behavior within the group. Little things that seemed to lend some sense of character or personality.

Some keep their spines rigid as they move while others writhe around, their torsos gone strangely slack so they seem to squirm like a snake with every step.

I watched one drag his face along the front window of a hardware store as he moved down a sidewalk, a smear trailing behind him the color of Baja Blast Mountain Dew. Did he like the way the glass felt, or was it just random behavior?

I'm not sure which answer I'd even prefer. Which notion is more disturbing – the idea of some animal order at play, some differentiation, some individuality between the members of this group of things, or the idea that all of their behavior truly is mindless, chaotic, utterly without meaning?

Shit. Which is worse?

When I think about these things, and when I look upon these walking corpses, I wonder what salvation we're promising people. Yes, we will have food and shelter, for now. Yes, we will have a community that we can hopefully keep safe for a time. But where's the path to a better world in hunkering down in cabins? Aren't we just marketing again? Selling them hopes and dreams that will never come true? I kind of thought I was done doing that. I hoped so, anyway.

-Ray

Fiona

Beckley, West Virginia
126 days after

I don't remember the exact sequence of events, don't recall the moment the feeling came over me or even what I might have been thinking. It's all a bit blurry, even if it was earlier tonight.

Doyle sat in the rocking chair, dumping more booze into his mouth. His face had settled into a resting scowl, I think from the harshness of the whiskey which had crept closer to room temperature.

I remember seeing him like an animal, if that makes sense. I saw him as a masculine creature for once instead of a sad dog, and I remember wanting him to do what I wanted him to, wanting to feel that power over him.

But I didn't want to see him during, didn't want to see the wet eyes or the juicy lips or the receding hairline. I knew that, so I blew out the lantern and candles before I made my move. The snow outside reflected enough light that I could still kind of see, at least here in the living room, though mostly just the shapes of things.

With the lights low, I threw a couple of logs onto the fire, the orange glow lighting up a wedge of the room as the door hung open. I could hear Doyle smacking his lips behind me, but I didn't look. I didn't want to see. The door squeaked shut, and the dark returned.

I sat down on the edge of the mattress and faced the shadow sitting in the rocking chair. He wasn't Doyle anymore, just a masculine silhouette. Any man. Every man.

I reached out for the dark figure, my fingers clasping his, and I pulled him to me. He sat on the edge of the bed beside me, and I directed his hands to my breasts, and I felt how excited he was, and I liked it. I liked that I could do this to him, that he had no real choice in the matter, that I must be obeyed.

The hiss of the burning wood picked up in the stove, and the heat intensified. I leaned away from him to peel my shirt off, and then his shirt was off, too, and we were two animals lying together, skin on skin, beads of sweat intermingling.

I felt his open mouth pressed into my shoulder, lips and the edges of teeth sliding over to my neck, and I didn't feel it as Doyle, and I didn't feel it as Warner. I felt it as every man. All of them at once, somehow.

The same for the sex itself. I didn't feel it as something we did together. I felt it as a power I had over him, dominion over a man, over every man, maybe. I pressed my hands into his face at the climax, muffling him, covering him up, blocking out his eyes and nose and mouth like he wasn't real, like I could just snuff him out and make him small if I wanted. Heat radiated from his blocked out face into my hands, slicked them with sweat. And this primal heat proved that I wasn't some helpless thing who watched her husband and children die one by one, that I still had power, that I still existed.

Fiona

Beckley, West Virginia
127 days after

Warner died on the toilet, shitting his guts out. He refused to
go to the hospital. Said it was already too late, and he'd rather
die at home. While I could identify with him and respect that
choice on a certain level, it didn't make for a pleasant time for
the family, during or after his dying days. I mean, I think we
all thought of his bloody spray and pained noises every time
we took a shower or brushed our teeth after that.

Of course, that wasn't long for the children. Within the
next three weeks they were all gone. It's too awful to write
about, though, too awful to even think about.

It's been months now, I guess, and I still feel like I just got
the wind knocked out of me, that little panicked twitch in my
chest like if I don't regain the ability to breathe soon, I'm not
going to make it either.

Everyone says life goes on, but to me it feels more like
death goes on. It goes on and on, and it never goes away.
Never gets any better.

Sometimes I think it's not so bad, the cold. If it kills some
of the stink in the city, I'll be happy.

I took a walk today, taking the trail that winds out around
the lake. Most of the snow melted this morning, though it had
gotten cold enough again later on in the afternoon that my

breath steamed from my nostrils all along the way. Usually by the time I get to the South side of the water, I can smell the sewage smell blowing in from the city where the pipes are all backed up. It's crazy if you go any closer than that. The paint literally peeled off of all the cinder block buildings from whatever combination of chemicals and excrement stenches fill the air. I'm guessing it's only a matter of time before it strips the wooden homes bare, too.

Anyway, today I smelled nothing like that, just the smell of the lake. The scent of the water always seems cleaner to me in the winter, too. Fresher.

The muscles in my legs tightened up about halfway in, got a little sore on me, but it felt good to get them some work. And there's something about that sound of the water lapping against the banks that never gets old. It's peaceful.

Lorraine

The Compound
111 days after

Ray,

Here's a question that will sound dumb: Do you think the dead will die off? I mean, can they stumble around rotting forever? Won't things start to fall off? Limbs, such as legs, that are mandatory for said stumbling to transpire?

If so, hunkering down for a while, even if it's a long while, really is the smartest move. Banding together in one place we can defend, stockpiling food and weapons in a location with a water supply. Sounds pretty good to me.

I think being out there on the road so much, you have a different perspective. Here, we work together all day. We pound nails side by side, work paint brushes up and down to seal the exposed wood of the steps and porches on the cabins. We cook and clean and log the scavenged supplies. We sit down together a couple times a day for meals.

We sweat together. We eat together. Something about those things bonds people like nothing else. As the days pass, we're more and more like a family. And even if you're not here for most of it, we talk about you. Everyone talks about you. The men and the women and the children. They all admire you. Admire that you brave a harsh world so more can share in our community.

That's the role you find yourself in. The one you were

born to play. This is our family now, and every family needs a father. I think you'll make a great one.

-*Lorraine*

Ray

Lorraine,

I am going to write this here, scrawl it on this page in black ink, and then we're never going to speak of it again. You will not ask me about it. Ever. And if you do, I will not answer. Not now. Not in a month. Not in ten years. I can't.

It was a little subdivision out away from town. Tract homes. Identical boxes in perfect rows like a mouth full of porcelain veneers.

I don't know what made me veer that way and drive around the loop. I pass bunches of these types of upper middle class mini-neighborhoods without checking. I'd never expect to find someone in one. They don't make much sense in terms of places to stay long term, you know? Those wide open lawns make for poor cover, and there are no good water sources around most of them, I'd guess.

I slowed down, creeping past the homes. I swiveled my head back and forth to peer into the gaps between the houses, as though someone, or something, might appear there, some figure tucked back in the shadows. Perhaps alive. Perhaps dead. I don't know what I expected, really. Nothing appeared there, of course. Nothing but overgrown grass that swayed in the breeze; bushes gone from tightly cropped to shaggy like unkempt beards.

And then I heard something. Or I thought I did. A high pitched whoop of some kind. I stopped the car. Put the window down. Listened.

Whatever it was, it had been muffled, hard to place. Hell, it was hard to even discern any specific characteristics. I wasn't even certain I'd heard anything.

I listened for a time, but it didn't repeat itself for my sake or anything. That would have been too easy, I guess.

I crept on, leaving the window down. Just in case.

I didn't think anything good would come of this. Still, even if there was the remotest chance that someone here needed my help, I had to pursue it somehow. That's what we've signed on for, the way I see it. I don't know.

A yellow house took shape ahead, set apart from the rest at the end of the loop. The vinyl siding had faded almost to white on one side where the sun had bleached it. A curved line beneath the eaves formed the border between yellow and white like a tan line on a boob.

My eyes locked onto the place as I approached, tracing down vinyl siding to the blue door, partially open, and then dancing a moment upon each window, only one of which was broken. Still, over and over again my eyes made their way back to that border where the white gave way to yellow.

The longer I looked at the place, the more it looked like one of those diagrams in the anti-crystal meth pamphlets at drug rehab facilities. The cartoon of the rotten teeth with the rim of yellow and brown along the gum line. That was what happened before they crumbled away for good. My son described something like that to me once, a little less than a year before he passed. Biting down on an Everlasting

Gobstopper and feeling two molars splinter, shards of bone flaking onto his tongue just bigger than powder.

And then I heard it again. The sound. Close. It made the hairs on my neck prick up right away. I couldn't tell if it was coming from inside the yellow house, but it seemed likely.

The only words I can think to describe it are "scream" and "screech," but neither of them are quite right. They don't do the noise justice. It sounded shrill and harsh like a woman screaming hard enough to shred her vocal cords, but it had an insectile quality to it as well. Almost like when cicadas get to chirping real loud.

I couldn't tell if it was pained or aggressive. Either one seemed totally possible, and for some reason, I had to know which it was.

I eased into the driveway and killed the engine, my gun out and clenched in my hand, the muzzle resting against my knee. I waited there in the silence for a long moment. Listening. Hearing nothing.

Clouds passed in front of the sun just then, and shade fell over everything. The shadows stretched down from beneath the eavestrough, darkness creeping down past that borderline onto the white.

Finally, I stepped out of the car, closing the door with care so it gave back just a little click. Nothing loud enough for anyone, or anything, to notice. I hoped.

I stood a while, a long while, feet planted on the concrete of the driveway, shoulders squared to the house. I watched the crack where the door stood open, half expecting some hint of movement, some little jerk or sway to betray the person standing behind it. But no. No movement. No person. I knew that. Sort of.

Beads of sweat sluiced down the back of my neck, sogging into my collar. I wiped what I could away with my hand, knowing more droplets would form to replace their fallen brethren. I dried my palm on the thigh of my pants and looked at the dark smear there a moment before my gaze returned to the yellow house.

I moved toward it, finally, not realizing until I was in motion how sick I felt. My guts knotted themselves up, the tangle of pink ropes in my middle cinching into a cramped ball of muscle. I get that when I'm nervous, that kind of overwhelming nausea that seems to creep into more and more intense territory and makes it impossible to sit still.

I stayed light on my feet, but the soles of my shoes still scuffed against the sidewalk, a tiny patter that made my neck and shoulders tense.

I pushed the door and watched it glide away from me in slow motion. It squealed as it swung, a high pitched tone that got deeper as it tapered away to silence.

A landing took shape in the gloom just beyond the open doorway, with a staircase leading up to the right and another leading down to the left. The house was a split level.

I waited a beat, forced myself to breathe normally, to fight whatever impulse implored me to take shallow breaths. A tingle rippled over my scalp. Even with these physical signs of panic coming upon me, though, my thoughts remained clear.

I stepped up and through the doorway, my shoulders twitching once as the shade surrounded me. The air was cool and dry, harsh in my throat and against my lips. The feel of it made me acutely aware that I was in a different space, like I'd somehow traveled more than the few steps from the front stoop to this landing; I'd left one world behind and entered another when I pushed open that blue door and crossed that threshold.

After a moment's hesitation, I started up the steps. I don't know why I decided to go upstairs first. I think I was sick of stalling more than anything. Time to rip off the damn band-aid and be done with it.

The carpet seemed plush, perhaps freshly installed just before it all went to hell. For the time being I didn't like the way it scrunched under my feet. It made me feel vulnerable, like I didn't have the grip, the level of control, I normally would.

The quiet swelled to a nothing scream around me. So silent it made my heart beat faster, made my eyes jerk and twitch to look over everything. Nothing stirred in the dining room and kitchen ahead of me as I neared the top of the stairs, though the wall wrapped around a corner into a hallway to my left that I couldn't see down from my vantage point.

The floorboard groaned as I reached the top step, and after a beat, a deep thump resonated from somewhere down that hallway. The second sound seemed a response to the first, I thought, a reaction to the creaking floor.

My mouth dropped open without my say so, and the dry air clawed at my throat. I swallowed, my epiglottis clicking, the saliva creeping down my esophagus like moisture soaking into a dried out sponge. It seemed dead, this air.

The shadows fluttered in the light beneath the door at the end of the hall. The dark spots shifted to the side and disappeared, leaving only the glow spilling out from the next room.

It was hard to fathom, the notion of a creature stirring just on the other side of this rectangle of wood. It was disturbing in some way. Whether it was living or dead almost didn't matter. It didn't feel right.

I inched that way, my eyes fastened to that semi-circle of brightness shining under the door. I stayed light on my feet. Soundless.

The gun rose in front of me, and the black hunk of metal quivered for a second as my arm moved it into place. It felt alive in my hand. A throbbing organism that made my palm tingle. I could feel how it was just waiting to go off.

I don't remember deciding to speak, but the words came out of my mouth anyway, my voice sounding deeper and more gravelly than I remembered.

"If you're in there, and you're alive, say something now. Otherwise, I'm coming in blasting."

Another thump. Another flitter of shadows undulating in the light beneath the door.

I waited long enough to take a single deep breath, arms and fingers prickling with the adrenaline, and then I kicked the door down. It cracked like a baseball bat hitting the ball cleanly, wood splintering around the latch. The thing swung a quarter of the way open and stopped abruptly as it struck whatever had been standing just beyond it, the whole thing shivering on the recoil like a tuning fork.

I kicked it again, more of a push to try to knock the thing off balance. It worked. I felt the door push something down with a sound like a 40 pound bag of salt getting dropped on the floor.

I sidled through the opening then, the gun pointing the way in front of me.

Sunlight streamed through the windows, the light seeming bright white somehow after my time in the hallway. Almost like the light in a hospital room.

The thing squirmed on the floor like a beetle stuck on its back, arms and legs moving without clear purpose, seemingly trying random combinations of motions in hopes that one would right it. Noises jabbered out of his mouth as he flailed.

It was a boy. A dead one. Maybe high school age. Shirtless with a black crater in the center of his chest. A ragged wound scabbed up into a rough texture almost like the blackened remains of a log after a campfire.

I raised the gun and shot him in the head, and the kicking and jabbering cut off all at once.

I looked on the thing for a beat, but I felt nothing in particular. It was the first one I'd killed since Arkansas.

I turned and stepped through the doorway, reentering the shade of the hall.

And then the screaming started again. Somewhere ahead of me.

Fiona

Beckley, West Virginia
128 days after

Doyle stood in the doorway with another wagon load of wood behind him. It was the first time he'd stopped by since it happened, and he struggled to maintain eye contact, blinking and looking at the floor, eyeballs juiced up even wetter than usual. His hair looked more frazzled than normal, too, puffs of it half-feathered up from the wind.

"Brought a little more wood since the snow cleared out."

"Thanks. Come on in."

He nodded and wheeled the wagon in. I stood back and watched as he went to work stacking the wood in front of the blanketed up sliding door. He spoke with his back turned, those wisps of frizzy hair bobbing as his head moved.

"Better to get as much lumber as we can in here before the snow settles in to stay a while. That's the way I figure it."

"Yeah, that makes sense."

His spine and shoulder blades sidled back and forth in front of me, and the pieces of wood clattered into each other as they moved from the wagon to the stack. It sounded like that slow clapping that builds into thunderous applause, except it didn't go anywhere. It stayed slow.

"You think you'd like to stay-"

"I better get going early tonight. It smells like snow again, and I'm beat from splitting wood all day. Arms and back are pretty tender just now, you know?"

He still stood with his back to me, but his head sunk down now, facing the floor, almost disappearing behind his shoulders. Everything fell quiet for a long moment. Totally still.

"I understand."

He turned to face me, his eyes only meeting mine for a fraction of a second before he brought a hand up to rub his index finger and thumb at them. He took a breath and his chest quivered a little.

I couldn't believe how rattled he seemed. Usually he was so chatty, yakking my ear off about the minutiae of his day. He didn't even mention that it was Thanksgiving. I guess I'm glad I didn't cook anything.

After a beat, he strode to the door, his hand still blocking his eyes, and then he spoke over his shoulder.

"Well, it was good to see you. I'll try to bring more wood along soon, weather permitting."

"Thanks, Doyle."

He stepped over the threshold and closed the door behind him. I heard the spring creak as the screen door swung closed and click as it latched, and I watched through those two panes of glass as Doyle's back moved away from the house.

He never looked back.

I tossed and turned on the mattress for a long while, but sleep refused to overtake me. Lying there wasn't wholly unpleasant, though. I found a little peace, if not slumber. I listened to the fire's breath, and the sound of the wood cracking periodically, and the wind blowing over the stovepipe chimney with a low pitched whistle that sounded like a cross between someone blowing across the top of a beer bottle and some freighter's fog horn out at sea.

My spine stretched out, all of the muscles in my back letting go one by one, the tissue around each vertebrae sighing in relief, the lack of tension bringing me pleasure.

My body rested some, but my mind couldn't. So I got up and lit a couple of candles, went out to the porch to get the jar of water I put out there. I never realized how much I'd miss having cold drinking water on tap until it was gone. Oh, it's cold when it comes straight out of the well, but once I haul the buckets in, it gets up to room temp before long. I leave big mason jars on the porch often to keep it chilled, though I know they'll start to freeze over here soon. Maybe by then the rooms at the back of the house will be cold enough to do the job, which would make for a mixed blessing.

Doyle tumbled around in my thoughts as I tried to sleep, of course. The man confuses me now more than ever. His behavior earlier today was hard to figure, that was for sure. Even now, I see his back to me when I close my eyes. It feels like wherever he is out there, his back is surely to me. Strange. Something about our sexual encounter disturbed him or made him uncomfortable around me.

Did he feel guilty about something? Perhaps. That could explain it. His wife died two and a half years ago of breast cancer, however, so his guilt wouldn't be out of any sense of marital betrayal, or at least I wouldn't think so.

With anyone else, I could buy it as more of a general awkwardness, some shyness or embarrassment bubbling up to the surface, but Doyle didn't seem that type to me. The guy had always been a talker, totally unashamed.

Frustrating.

It's strange to write in the dark. The candle on my desk flickers when I exhale through my nostrils, and the shadows flit across the paper of this notebook.

The dark falls so early now, and the nights last so long. I better go put some wood in the stove and try to sleep.

Fiona

Beckley, West Virginia
130 days after

Another two days have come and gone without sign of Doyle.
I vacillate between frustration and worry. Sometimes I think
about walking the nine blocks down to his place to check on
him, but it seems a little forward.

The snow refrained from really falling the past two nights.
The sky spit tiny flakes now and then, but nothing that
accumulated. Still, it's been cold as hell. Painful when the
wind blows.

My hands wear flaked up red spots from the trips back
and forth getting water. They're rough to the touch like the
texture of the sidewalk. Cracks branch over my lips, too. It
hurts like hell to smile. Not that there's been much to smile
about for a long time. Even the unexposed places are starting
to go now. The skin on my back feels papery, flaky, dried out.

I'm burning through my wood faster than I'd hoped, too.
I've tried to take it slow, tried to keep the fire simmering
instead of blazing, but I think it burns faster now that the air
is so dry.

I dreamed of Doyle. Of our torsos pressed together in the
dark, skin on skin, moist with sweat as thick as vegetable oil.
His hands and arms trembled where they touched me, and
my skin prickled in those places as well, a feeling like

goosebumps with the electricity cranked up, every follicle roiling.

And the tingle spread throughout my body, crawling up to the top of my head, creeping down between my thighs. I felt it in my breath, in the tips of my fingers, in all of those tiny places between my teeth.

And I leaned back atop him, sitting upright so I towered over him, over the shape of him in the dark. Our bodies moved in unison, and I felt that power again, of all of his energy channeled into worship of me, of his will slaved to my command. And it didn't feel like he pressed himself into me. It felt like I was consuming him. I didn't accept him. I tamed him, controlled him, ingested him.

I brought a hand to the pillow beneath his skull, and I took it, pulling it out from under. With both hands, I nestled it down onto his face with care, compressing inch by inch until his breathing cut off. I held it there for a long time, held it as the bucking of his hips under me weakened, held it until he went still piece by piece, finally releasing it when the rise and fall of his chest had ceased for some time.

I stayed there, straddling the still figure. He was so entranced that he never even fought back. He submitted to my command until the end.

Fiona

Beckley, West Virginia
133 days after

The snow shrouds everything in white. Huge flakes drift down to find their place among the others, all of them joining on the ground or on rooftops, attaching so the many become one. Others latch onto branches and dead power lines, encasing them in puffy sleeves.

The flakes fall now as they have for the past six hours without pause. The speed has changed some, the rate of snowfall speeding and slowing like someone flipping that switch on the windshield wipers. At its thickest, I couldn't really see the house across the street through the white haze. It's not far from that even still, more like looking through the flakes and some kind of gray wisps at the house over there.

We're up to six inches of accumulation and counting, and I know in my bones that it won't let up for a long while.

So that's it. No more waiting around. I guess it's here. The real winter. The snow that stays for keeps.

So quiet now out there. I went to fill a couple of buckets of water, and the snow muffled all of the sound. Muted it. It wasn't just quieter, though. The sound seemed different fundamentally. Dryer and darker and duller. Despite the idea of the snow absorbing some of the volume, it was so still out there that my every movement seemed blaring, obnoxious, downright attention-seeking against the starkness.

The snow drifted up against the house, and that which was left flat on the ground turned brittle with a crusted top like crème brule. With every step, I snapped through that crisp layer, sinking just beyond ankle deep in the fluff. The crunch of every footstep rang out as I trudged through it, buckets dangling at my sides.

I cranked the pump, metal squawking against metal, shrill and harsh like a wounded bird. My heart fluttered before the fear wormed its way into my consciousness. The worst feeling crept over me just then like I wasn't alone, like I was being watched. I wanted to keep going, to keep yanking the crank up and down like it was nothing, like it was all in my imagination, but I couldn't.

I stopped. The crank slowed to a halt, and I let my hand fall away from the handle. I watched the steam twirl out of my nostrils, and when my exhale ended, I held my breath. Listened. The few drops of water plunking into the bottom of the bucket provided the only sound.

Someone was behind me somewhere, I knew. Someone watching. Waiting. Someone laughing at my fear.

I tried to block out my grandma's words about the dark figure who would rule over those left behind on an empty world, about the antichrist, but I couldn't do it.

My neck throbbed, quivered like an overfilled water balloon about to burst. My shoulders twitched, fighting my command to turn around, to face what must be behind me.

I tottered from foot to foot, that hardened layer of snow cracking and crunching out sounds like someone chewing on ice cubes. My vision twirled away from the pump, passing over the yard and facing the street behind me.

Nothing.

No one.

The same empty houses, empty town, empty world as always. Total isolation.

The wind picked up, and the snow blew around, kicking up from the ground in swirls of white powder. When the light hit the icy bits in the air, they twinkled like glitter.

I filled the buckets and went back inside.

I find myself disturbed. Too disturbed to sleep. When I close my eyes I see myself standing at the pump, slowly turning to face the emptiness. I see the vacant houses all around me. I see the snow whipping around, swells of it curling and disintegrating in the air.

A thought wriggles in my head like an Earthworm on a rainy sidewalk. What if someone really was there when I was getting the water earlier? What if Doyle was the one watching me? Is that possible?

Fiona

Beckley, West Virginia
136 days after

The drifts lean into the doors and the sides of the house. It
looks like a bunch of white waves crashed into the building
and got frozen in place. More like time itself stopped mid-
crash rather than the freezing being temperature based.

The drifting makes it harder to estimate how much snow
has fallen out there. It's a lot. I'd say somewhere in the 18-24
inch range. The drift against the front door is probably three
and a half feet. Ridiculous.

Of course, the snow stopped, finally, after a day and a half,
and it only got colder out there. The kind of cold that freezes
that little bit of moisture in my nostrils as soon as I set foot
outside.

The cracks on my hands look like spider webs now, too,
and papery flaps of skin dangle from my nostrils. I have to
stop myself from picking them off, because that only makes it
sting and get worse, turning all red and mottled.

A week has come and gone without Doyle checking in. I
know the snow makes travel difficult, but I thought he'd want
to make sure I was OK. I thought he'd want to see me.

I lie here and listen to the wind swishing the snow around.
Sometimes, if it blows just right, the smoke plumes down
from the chimney to swirl around by the window. I watch it
through the glass, watch it dip and twirl and float up and

away. It almost feels like watching something on TV.

I sat by the stove, sipping whiskey in the dark. Not to get drunk so much as to feel that burn on my lips, feel it spiral down my throat like chemicals going down the drain, smarting all the way down.

I took the bottle straight to my face, clenching the glass between my teeth and tipping it back. No reason to bother with drinking glasses now, I figured. There was no one left to try to impress.

The fire had burned down, though there was plenty of heat in the room. Still, it was quiet without that constant hiss all around me. The wind still blew now and then, sprinkles of snow whipping into the windows and siding, but these sounds only served to remind me of the quiet.

My consciousness seemed to whittle down to just those few elements. The dark. The quiet. The feel of the bottle against my lips. The burn of the alcohol catching in my throat.

In time, that alcoholic tingle crept into my head, crept into my thoughts, and things came clear the way they can only when you've been drinking. The disconnected pieces snaked their way together to form new thoughts, fresh perspectives.

I thought about how the nights are long and dark, the space between the days stretching out into something unpleasant. It almost felt like a new day would never actually arrive, like when you hold your breath underwater just long enough that a panicked feeling overtakes you, like some part of you already believes after 45 seconds that you'll never draw breath again.

And then I thought of Doyle. I saw him delivering big wagon loads of wood, stacking them for me. I thought about how he did all of these favors for me right up until he got me in bed, and then they cut off and he vanished. Maybe that should have been obvious all along, but I didn't think of it that way until tonight, the idea that sex was his end game all the while, that he used me.

I thought about how eerie it had been for all that time, the way he always knew just when to bring wood, just when to do whatever I needed. Strange, right? Not only was he the last man on Earth, he also seemed to read my thoughts.

What were the chances of that, anyway? That it would be just the two of us left here in town? That everyone else would die or leave, and just the two of us would remain here and meet up? And how did we wind up in bed when I was repulsed by him like I was? How did things go this way? Looking back, it seemed such an unlikely course of events.

And I thought about what all of that might mean going forward. Were we just left here to do as the devil pleased, confused and flailing, perpetually confounded by our own behaviors? Did the antichrist set me on this strange path that seemed to make no sense to me? Did he hold sway over my thoughts even now?

I tried to picture Doyle there in the room with me, just sitting in the rocking chair in front of the window in the dark, just that outline of him, that silhouette of a man there that I could just barely make out. I tried to imagine what I'd say to him if he were there. I wasn't sure.

And then I remembered that moment by the pump, that

awful moment when I knew in my heart that someone was watching me, that Doyle was watching me, and all of these puzzle pieces snapped together.

He read my thoughts. He spied on me and bent me to his will, used me for his pleasure. It was him. It had to be. Everyone else died. Everyone died but me and the antichrist.

Fiona

Beckley, West Virginia
137 days after

I woke in the dark, hung over, my tongue a piece of fine grit sandpaper glued to the roof of my mouth. My thoughts had cleared some, the clouds of drunkenness parting.

A determined feeling had taken root as I slept. In my brain. In my heart. It steeled me. Calmed me. Prepared me for what might come next.

I opened the stove and prodded around with the fire poker. A few coals flickered orange when I moved them, but it was almost all the way out. I piled in a handful of skinnier logs and a couple of crumpled up phone book pages, and the flames kicked up a little.

I liked the way the orange light shined on my face as the paper burned, liked the way the heat swelled in time, the way it felt upon my cheeks and the bridge of my nose. The glow lurched and faded and brightened at random like a living, squirming thing.

I crumpled more balls of phone book paper, tossing them in as needed to keep the fire licking into the wood until it had time to catch. The yellow paper balls unfurled as the flames consumed them, ads for cleaning services going black and breaking up into ashy flaps.

I knew in some way that I couldn't be sure. Not yet, anyway. I couldn't know with certainty that Doyle was the destroyer, the beast, the one who orchestrated all of this disease and death. If I were going to act on it in some way, I needed proof.

I closed my eyes, the glow of the fire flickering against my eyelids.

If it were him, he would be marked, wouldn't he? Some marking on his skin, likely on his forehead or on the back of his hand. I recalled reading that. Maybe that would provide the truth I needed.

The wood blackened along the edges, smoke twirling off of it, thick and white. Soon it would burn like all the rest.

I slept off and on throughout the morning, the light in the room creeping to a brighter shade of gray each time I woke. It was the best I've slept in a long while. I needed the rest.

The fire had burned down somewhere in there, and the cold closed in on me. The lack of warmth outside of my blankets made it almost impossible to muster the willpower to climb out of bed, but I did it.

I pulled on three pairs of socks before crossing the wood floor to the back of the house, but the chill fought its way up through to shock my heels and toes, numbing them right away.

I ladled a mug of water out of the bucket and brushed my teeth. This act woke me up the rest of the way, and I realized how much better I felt. How that sting in my eyes had retreated, how clear my thoughts had become. Weird how it sneaks up on you once in a while, how good it feels to be alive. Rinsing my mouth out with frigid water only cemented the sensation.

I was ready to make my move.

Ray

Rural Virginia
111 days after

The screech erupted somewhere ahead of me, somewhere in the shade. Shrill and dry and close. I froze, looked for movement in the shadows.

The gun ascended before me again, quivering at the end of my arm. My hand and forearm went icy and numb, and my arm seemed more like something hovering there than an actual part of me.

I opened my eyes wider, trying to will my pupils into adjusting to the lack of light here. Still, I saw nothing. No movement. Just the vague outline of the dining table and chairs beyond the mouth of the hallway, solid black shapes that stood out against the gray everywhere else.

I crept forward, neck and forehead slicked with sweat, jaw muscles bunching and releasing in fast speed, teeth gritting without my say so. My heart quaked in my chest so hard that my ribcage rattled a little with every beat.

Entering the shade felt like I was being submerged in something physical, the darkness touching my clammy skin, pressing itself into me like it'd leave black marks all over. Still, I eased forward, feet skimming over that plush carpet, the end of the hallway ever nearer.

Another scream. It sounded so close, so loud, that it was hard to believe it wasn't right on top of me, that it must be somewhere out there in the dark instead of inches from me. I couldn't quite accept that notion, kept waiting for something with claws to leap out of nowhere like a pouncing cat to attach itself to my face.

I crossed the line where the hall ended and the walls opened up into the kitchen and dining room. I scanned the new terrain, head swiveling back and forth. Still nothing moving, no being present that I could see.

I could now see a rectangle of illumination where sunlight spilled out from behind curtains to my right. Not enough to light the space too much, but it somehow felt better to have that little source of light rather than the darkest shade of the hallway.

I took a few steps forward, stopping just shy of the dining table. Once again my voice caught me off guard. I didn't feel myself choosing to speak, didn't think of the words before they came out, and my voice itself sounded grittier than usual.

"Whoever, or whatever, the fuck you are, best come out now."

The curtains fluttered like giant wings, flapping and parting in the middle, the bottom billowing up like a parachute. The opening between the drapes widened, and the light flooded into the room, spilling over the table and chairs which stood between me and the window.

In the confusion, all I could think was that a bird had come through the broken window and couldn't find the way out, flitting about, squawking periodically. It would make sense, I thought.

Then the silhouette stepped into the opening between the curtains. The outline of a boy, maybe 8 or 10 years old, arms thrashing to free himself from the fabric still partially draped over him. He froze then, light streaming to light up his messy hair from behind, arms still raised over his head. His shoulders jerked once and held still again. I thought maybe this was as he saw me, a recoil of shock or fright, but being backlit, his face was entirely encased in shadow from my vantage point, so I didn't know what to think.

He screamed like a wild animal then, like some human-insect hybrid tipping his head back to howl and chirp and screech all at once.

The hair on the back of my neck stood on end, and goosebumps prickled and tingled all up and down my limbs. I could tell by the sound that he wasn't dead, wasn't some mindless resurrection case like the others. But then I didn't think he was quite right, either.

I shuffled back a few steps without thinking about it, without thinking about anything, the gun wavering from side to side in front of me. My left shoulder blade collided with the corner where the room tapered to a hallway, the contact making me jump, all of those tingling places throbbing with terror and ice and adrenaline.

The boy charged at me, an animal now more than a human, the way I saw him, a beast growing darker and grayer as it jolted away from the window's light and fully immersed itself into the shaded part of the room.

The gray blur zigzagged around the table and chairs, and I traced his serpentine path with the gun as best I could. The muscles in my arm shook like hell, and I heard my breath whistling between my clenched teeth.

I didn't know what to do. I didn't know what to think.

When he got close, my finger tightened on the trigger.

He jumped.

I squeezed.

The muzzle blazed, lighting up his face and my shaking hand in orange for a split second. Then the crack of the gunfire split the air around us open. The gun kicked just a touch against the crook of my hand.

And his head came apart. It almost looked like the bullet popped open the top of his skull like a lid for just a second and poured the contents out. I know that can't be what happened, but when I try to remember it, that's what I see. The rounded top slides up just a touch and the red and the bits spill out.

Jesus. I put a bullet in a little boy's skull.

The brains and blood hit the floor first like some jelly and cream cheese concoction belly smacking the carpet. A wet slap. Heavy. The body made impact a moment later, hitting the ground limp. With a thud. Dead weight. Literally.

And the blood drained out for a little while, pooling around the broken head, darkening the red carpet in a semi-circle. The bleeding verified it. He had been alive. Not the black goop that seeps out of the dead ones, this was red blood.

I went to the window and opened the curtains the rest of the way. I don't know why.

The sunlight lit up everything. Motes of dust swirled over the table where the whoosh of the moving curtains had kicked them up. The sun glared off of each one like a handful of glitter floated over me. Over us. All of the shiny pieces drifted away from me and moved toward the body.

And now I saw the boy in full color. He looked lean and

hard for such a young kid. Tan, too. A scar etched a crooked pink line into one cheek, and scabs seemed to trace the circular lines where the eyes and cheekbones connected.

Had he survived out here alone? Had he gone a little mad in the process? Had he always been that way? A rabid child left out here with no one for miles? No one but the dead, that is.

But no. No more. I don't want to know.

We'll just leave it here in this letter, and we'll never touch upon it again. Not in text. Not out loud. Never again.

Sometimes it feels like that's our only choice, doesn't it? Both options flawed and awful. To stare into the wound, or to pretend it doesn't exist.

-Ray

Fiona

Beckley, West Virginia
137 days after

Bright white surrounded me, enough light to force my eyes down to the narrowest squint. I watched the world through the blur of my eyelashes, lifting my chin to look up. The sky opened up above me, endless empty space. Clear cold air that stretched from me to the gray wisps that shrouded the heavens.

I trudged through the snow, half jogging, my feet crunching through the crusted surface over and over. I almost felt bad to sully that white blanket covering the ground, to crash across the surface of it and rip it up.

Holes gouged the ground with each step, pocking that sprawl of snow. The footprints themselves made me uneasy as well, a trail of hard evidence displaying where I'd been, hinting at what I was up to. A dotted line that led straight to me. So I ran in slow motion behind the houses in the subdivision, moving right along the tree line where the backyards gave way to the woods rather than traveling on the sidewalk or road. Maybe I couldn't conceal the prints very easily, but I could tuck them away. Keep them places his eyes were less apt to go.

The snow grabbed my feet and ankles with each step. It made sure I worked twice as hard to get half as far, made sure that my best attempt at running still resulted in sloth-like speeds.

My breath coiled in the air before me, plumes twirling out of my nostrils and trailing off to the sides as I rushed forward. It felt good to move in the open like this after so long confined to my little area. I felt like a dog getting loose for the first time in a long while, sprinting across the yard, leaping a few times for good measure.

My spine stretched out, and my arms pumped at my sides. I hurdled my way over and through the snow, launching myself into high steps that fell into a rhythm in time. From a distance maybe it would have looked like skipping more than hurdling. Kind of a moot point since everyone is dead. There was no one left to watch me from a distance.

The subdivision ended, but I still had a few blocks to go. I veered left into an alley, zigging and zagging through the yards that had no fences.

When I got within a block of Doyle's place, the crunch of my footsteps seemed louder. More obnoxious. More obvious. I slowed. Even my breathing seemed loud at that point. A little ragged. I felt the cold air abrade my throat as it sucked down into my chest. Something so strange about that chill getting inside of me, puffing up my lungs like two balloons filled with some foreign, cold gas.

I stopped. Stood perfectly still, my hands on my hips. I knew it made no real sense, but I wanted to get my breathing under control before I went any closer, wanted to feel in total command of my faculties as I made my move.

I imagined my face gone rosy in the cold, flushed, splotches and swirls of red everywhere. The flesh of my cheeks stung pretty good, a sensation that only made itself clear to me now that I was still. I guessed that the rush of air against my skin numbed that away as I jogged, but now I wielded no such protection from the pain. The sting swelled on cue, and when I grimaced, my dried out lips seemed to crack and split. I hoped it was my imagination.

My chest heaved a long time, spiraling the air in and out of me. Somehow the cold burned, the dry wind attacking all of the wet places inside of me, trying to make them crack as well. No amount of willpower could slow these breaths or quiet them. Somehow that alone made me want to panic, that feeling like my body disobeyed me, betrayed me, some irrational sense that my breathing might never slow to normal, might never quiet back down.

It did, though, of course, in time. I knew that I needed to remember that, to hold onto the notion of patience prevailing in these matters if I could.

I pressed forward, taking careful steps now. Quiet steps. A tingle throbbed in my chest, icy electricity palpitating within my ribcage. No matter how uneasy it might have made me, no matter how scared I might have been, there was something incredibly stimulating about sneaking up on Doyle like this, of turning the tables, of stalking him like my prey rather than the inverse.

The snow squeaked and cracked below me still, tiny versions of the thunderous bursts of sound that accompanied my jogging. The noises made my breath stutter in and out, the anxiety freezing my diaphragm, my body trying to stop and listen, an instinct I had to fight through just to walk and breathe at the same time.

There it was. Doyle's place. Brick and wood stained dark,

almost black, adorned the rear of the mid-century modern home. The nearly flat roof always made it look wide to me, sort of squat, and the rectangular windows were framed in lines that made them look much wider than they were tall, which probably accentuated the effect.

A decent sized back yard stood between me and the house. Much of the snow here was tramped down, especially that around the wood pile where an ax still stood at an angle, its head lodged into a log. Something about its trajectory reminded me of a tick sticking out of a dog's ear, growing fat with the blood of its host.

I swiveled my head to the left and right, scanning for a hiding spot that would provide the best vantage point. This was the tricky part, to get close enough to see without being detected or leaving footprints close enough to draw notice. There were a few trees to choose from, and some small brick structure coated in snow just beyond the wood pile. Maybe a little outdoor counter top for grilling? It was hard to tell with the few inches of white powder piled upon it.

It struck me that I wasn't even sure what I hoped to gain in this, at least not specifically. What could I possibly see from a distance that would clarify my position on these matters? What behavior could I observe that would confirm or deny my suspicions? And if the antichrist could read my thoughts, wouldn't he know what I was doing even before I did it?

Maybe, I thought, I was deluding myself. Maybe I had other reasons for spying on the man, or maybe I was losing it a little bit, my mind cracking and splitting and pulling apart in the cold just like the pink flesh of my lips. Maybe. It was hard to say, hard to think.

Something banged somewhere in front of me then, and my shoulders jerked in fright, that pang of electricity in my ribcage shooting panic all through me before I could think long enough to place the noise -- a door slamming shut. My eyes danced along the house, spotting a blurry silhouette rising up from the snow, a man with his back to me.

I ducked behind the closest tree.

Fiona

I held my breath. I listened, my ears straining to the point of sensing some high pitched ring that wasn't really there. Silence thrust itself at me, squirming everywhere around me in the air, screeching out shrill sounds that only existed in my head.

My shoulder scrunched into the bark of the tree where I leaned into it, pressing hard enough that I could feel the texture through my coat and hoodie and shirt. My knees bunched up into my chest. I brought a gloved hand up to my mouth, letting the side of my fist touch my lips.

Silence still rang out everywhere. Howling emptiness. Screaming nothing. I turned my head, trying to angle one ear and then the other toward the man, hoping at least one of them might hear something. Anything. Please.

And then his boots squeaked, crushing through the snow, beating down the packed areas as they moved. His gait seemed uneven. I couldn't imagine what might cause that, but the sounds grew louder, so I knew he was getting closer. Even with him advancing toward me, I felt better. Knowing where he was felt better.

I flicked my tongue out over those cracked and craggy flaps that used to be lips, regretting it right away when the opened up parts got to stinging, everything feeling that much colder when my tongue retracted, the frigidity latching onto the wet of my saliva. It felt like licking a tattering piece of cardboard and tasted salty, almost like tears in a strange way.

The pound of the footsteps stopped before they got all that close to me. After a beat of quiet, the snow squeaked again and a thud rang out of two solid objects colliding, with a second, softer collision following quickly after the first. Another beat of quiet. Another double thud, loud then quiet almost like a heartbeat.

I peaked around the corner in time to see the ax rise above the hatted head. It swung down, striking the quarter of a log sitting atop the block, splitting it long ways. The cleaved pieces tumbled to the ground on each side. He set the next piece of lumber down and repeated the process, gathering the split pieces every three or four passes and tossing them onto the wood pile.

Every inch of him looked to be gloved or hatted or otherwise swathed in winter attire, at least from my angle. This, of course, made it impossible to look for any telling marks or anything of that nature. Still, I watched him for a good long while, my mind teetering back and forth between the good or evil I might be gazing upon.

He lodged the ax in the block again and stood for a moment, hands on his hips. His shoulders rose and fell as he took deep breaths.

I sank back behind the tree trunk most of the way when he finally moved, tilting my head to the side so just that sliver of my head from the eyes up remained exposed.

He walked toward the house, grabbing something there near the door that I couldn't see, working it back and forth in the snow. It almost looked like a handle, maybe a different ax? A snow shovel? Whatever it was, it seemed to be stuck. He yanked on it, an awful scraping sound moaning out as he pulled it free.

He walked it out toward the wood pile, the handle dragging behind him, and then he moved into the clear where I could see it. The wagon. He grabbed arm loads of split wood and went to work stacking them into the bed of the wheeled cart.

He was loading wood to bring to me.

I stood without thought, hesitating for one second before I stepped out into the open, moving toward him. I crunched my way there, being loud on purpose so he'd hear.

His shoulders bunched as I got within a few paces. He froze a moment and then whirled to face me, in a crouched, almost karate stance, both arms hugging wood to his chest. A wild grimace wrinkled his face, eyes open far too wide, wet with fear.

"Oh, hey," he said, straightening up. "What are you doing out this way? I was just loading up some wood for you."

The wrinkles vacated his forehead and cheeks for the most part, though I could somehow still see where they'd been, a pale afterglow taking their place.

"I got sick of being cooped up," I said. "Decided to take a walk."

He squinted.

"You're bleeding."

"What?"

He pointed a puffy, gloved finger at me.

"Your lip. You're bleeding."

"Oh. Yeah, I'm pretty chapped."

I dabbed at my lips with my gloved fingers and checked them, though I couldn't make out any blood on the black fabric. It did look a little wet, though.

"It's flowing pretty good. Getting down onto your chin. Let's go inside and get you cleaned up."

Fiona

Beckley, West Virginia
137 days after

I filed into his house behind him, that mix of emotions doing cartwheels in my guts. Crossing the threshold felt so strange. It took my eyes a moment to adjust to the shade inside. He had blankets over most of his windows, too.

We peeled our boots off on a floor mat just inside the back door. Clumps of snow fell away from the sides of my boots, and inverted patterns of the treads remained where I'd taken my second to last steps. We headed into the kitchen.

I watched Doyle then, my eyes fastening to the fabric that concealed his hair line, waiting for that hat to come off. I'd never observed any kind of mark there before, but it's not like I was ever looking.

His hand gripped the knit hat, thumb and index finger pinching the front just above his eyebrows. He seemed to hesitate there, though, glancing at me out of the corner of his eye, perhaps noting the intensity with which I looked upon him. I turned my gaze to the floor, feeling weird. Feeling dumb.

It occurred to me that I had no idea what to think anymore. No idea. Nothing made any sense.

He turned away as he unsheathed that forehead, so I couldn't get a look at the front of his head, just his hair all frizzed up in the back from static electricity. He spoke as he walked off into a hallway.

"Have a seat. I'll get you something for that lip."

"Thank you."

I wasn't sure if he meant to head into the living room or to just take a seat on one of the stools at the snack bar next to us. I decided a little look around couldn't hurt, though.

I rounded the kitchen island and walked past the place he'd turned right, peering that way the best I could. The shade dominated the hallway he'd disappeared down. I could only really make out the mouth of the opening, the rest trailing away into black like some bear's den.

Wood squeaked under foot as I crossed the threshold into the living room. I paused for a moment, listening to see if he'd respond to the sound. He didn't, so I kept going.

Coals cracked and spit in the fireplace, one tiny flicker of flame still shimmering toward the back. A stack of dirty plates piled on the left hand side of the coffee table and used Kleenex and napkins congregated in clusters on the floor. So I had observed evidence of him being a slob, just not a demon.

His voice called from somewhere down the hall.

"You've got to be careful out in that cold. How long were you out there?"

"Not too long. It's always gone this way for me. Sensitive skin, especially my lips."

I scanned the room again, no real idea of what I could be looking for. What evidence might someone leave around hinting at their antichrist-ness? I didn't know. A warmth saturated my cheeks just then. Maybe part of it was the heat kicking out of the furnace, but I think it was mostly embarrassment. It felt silly to be performing this search.

His footsteps clattered down the hall toward me, the carpet muffling the sound a bit. He emerged from the mouth of that cave, his eyes swiveling from the kitchen into the living room to find me.

"Ah. Here you go."

He wiggled a little container of salve at me.

"Aloe Vera lip balm. Always helps my chapped lips heal up."

I padded over and took it from his outstretched arm. Everything went into slow motion as the jar transferred from his fingers to mine, my eyes locked on the discolored spot on the back of his right hand.

I gasped, unable to remove my hands from the pale region there.

"What? What is it?"

My heart fluttered in my chest, uneven and sloppy like a giant moth with soggy wings. My panicked brain struggled for words.

"Hm? Oh. Just... I must be seeing things in the dark here. It looked like your... like you had something... on your hand. The back of it, I mean."

"Hm? Oh, right."

He held up his hand so the back faced me, that pale square coming into focus a little better so I could see what it was.

"Burned myself heating a kettle over the fire. Heh. Bandage must have looked weird in the half-light or something."

"Yeah. It caught me off guard is all. Sorry about that."

He smiled, lips peeling back to reveal those strange teeth, and I tilted my head toward the object in my hands. I fumbled with the jar, fingers struggling to grip the lid and twist it open. Anything to not look at him any longer.

Fiona

Beckley, West Virginia
137 days after

I set the pot of water on top of the stove and sat down on the edge of the mattress to wait for it to warm up. The bottom sizzled where a rivulet of water had spilled down as I ladled it in. Just the sound of that, the hiss of the water droplet dancing across the top like a griddle, made me feel warmer. Of course, the noise of the fire raging within the stove didn't hurt either, I'm sure.

I felt ashamed. Ashamed that I'd let him fool me, let him touch me. Ashamed that even now part of me wanted to believe he was as he had appeared before, that the notion of his evil was some delusion.

Anyway, I got the overwhelming urge to clean myself after walking about in that demon's nest, and I spent the whole walk home dreaming about the shower I couldn't take, feeling all the little streams from the shower head flowing into the back of my neck, the heat draining down my spine, feeling the steam saturate the air around me, but no. No shower. Just a sponge bath. It took too long to heat up all the water necessary for a real bath, and I imagine it'd sting my hands something awful to soak in hot fluid at this point anyhow.

He tried to walk with me, tried to drag that wagon of wood along behind him in the snow, but it wasn't possible. Snow caked the wagon wheels and frosted the front of the wagon bed with a thick, smooth layer like butter cream on red velvet. I told him I had enough wood for now, and that he could bring it in a while when things melt a little. If they do.

I was glad to be rid of him, glad to look away, to walk away, but my skin itched the whole way home, aching for the scald of the sponge. A queasy feeling gurgled in my gut once I got out of sight of his place, and my hands tingled, vibrating from palm to fingertip. I knew then that my adrenaline had been going crazy that whole time, and now the after effects had come clear to me once the stimulation of being near him faded.

It wasn't until I got home and took my coat off that I realized that I'd sweat through everything, dark stains in oval shapes stretching down from each arm pit in both my t-shirt and sweatshirt. The inside of my coat soaked to the touch, the whole thing heavy with moisture, limp and sagging from the end of my arm like a soggy towel.

I lay back, my head resting on a bunched up blanket chunk, and I closed my eyes. The pot creaked a little bit on the stovetop, a sound that reminded me of cooking something on a real range. I pictured it, the wooden spoon stirring a sauce, mushrooms swirling in marinara, while a pot of water boiled on the burner next door, ready for the noodles. That's all I wanted. A shower and some homemade pasta. And I couldn't have either.

It seemed strange just then, the things we centered our lives around before. I had enough food to get by for this winter and a little beyond, at least. Doyle and I had scavenged a bunch of dried beans and oats, cans of various soups, even a bunch of boxes of Jello mixture and divided everything up.

And yet, foods I missed occurred to me constantly, delicacies and novelties I desired, everything from the simplest snacks to elaborate multiple course meals in fine dining restaurants. It seemed like food was no longer simply fuel to survive in my imagination. It was a confection, a fantasy made real, like before this my whole life was lived as a kid in a candy store, stuffing my face with disgusting sweet. And even with everyone dead, the dream remained the same, the gluttony remained. I missed all of those chips and crackers and chocolates that I didn't need as dearly as I missed anything.

My thoughts drifted out for a time, going quiet in the warmth, and then I pictured a candy store, the racks of colorful bags and boxes from floor to ceiling. All of those strange sugary products wearing their logos and brand names with pride. Candy bars and wafers and individually wrapped fruit chews that tasted nothing like real fruit.

And then I sat up, my eyes snapping open. I blinked a few times, eyes flitting over the pot on the stovetop. It hadn't reached a boil yet, not even close by the looks of it, but that was OK. I knew what I needed to do.

Fiona

The scene felt like a repeat of the afternoon before. The same pot sat on the stove, and the same sizzle hissed out from under it, but this time beige goop pooled where the water had been, and a wooden spoon drew invisible figure eights in the fluid. I lifted the spoon from the murk and tapped it on the side of the pot a few times, sheets of lumpy broth falling away with each hit.

Soup. Lentil soup. Not the most romantic of meals, I suppose, but it was enough of a draw to entice Doyle into coming over. I really stressed the positives: that it would be a hot meal that he wouldn't have to lift a finger toward cooking. Maybe that sold it more than the particular dish. Or maybe he was impressed that I trudged all the way there through the snow again just to invite him to dine with me.

Of course, I'd poisoned the hell out of it. See, that was the thing I had realized about Doyle. He didn't deserve to draw breath. Not anymore. He deserved a home cooked bowl of death with a cremation in the backyard for dessert.

Strychnine. Old rat poison that we've had in the garage for years. From what I've read about the stuff, it's a rough way to go. His death will be a painful one. I guess I'll have to find a way to hold back the tears.

I looked down upon the pot, the perfect circle of khaki

70

colored food. The smooth surface rippled when I dipped the spoon in once more and stirred so the bottom wouldn't scorch. Its scent wafted up at me, and it smelled good. Good enough to make my mouth water. None for me, though, thank you. Strychnine gives me terrible heartburn.

I left it to cook a while then, sitting on the corner of the mattress and laying back, letting my spine stretch out. I lay width ways so my legs dangled off one side of the bed and my head dangled off the other, my neck going limp and reveling in the lack of tension for a moment.

Little popping sounds rang out when bubbles formed and burst along the surface of the soup. With no way to control the heat, I'd have to remember to stir it soon to avoid that layer of skin forming along the top and bottom of it, all gummy and pasty and strange.

For now, I would rest, though. I would enjoy the way the strain lifted from my neck and back and shoulders for a long moment. As long as I could, anyway. It felt good to lie motionless, to go all limp, to rest my eyes. I hadn't slept much the night before, visions of entrees and poisons tumbling around in my head. I'd considered a variety of meals to serve as the poison's delivery system, but the lentil soup seemed like the best bet to mask any strange flavors. I could just layer in some spices to cover anything over.

Panicky feelings washed over me periodically. Notions that perhaps he would know what I was up to, that perhaps the beast was immortal or invincible in some way. But I reminded myself of what I had to lose. Nothing. If he didn't die, so be it, but I couldn't see any harm in trying. I couldn't see any other path at all.

I remembered the sound of the rats gnawing on the rafters in the garage, the smell of their piss. Years ago. In a different world than this. We tried to trap them first, shoving live traps up through the circular openings for the recessed light fixtures. We caught one or two, but the gnawing continued and the smell only got worse. We called an exterminator, and he tried a couple of things, killed a couple more, but it didn't help. More scuffing and gritting and gnawing up there. More piss.

When rat shit appeared in the pantry, I decided to get the poison. I hated to do it, but rodents can carry diseases that are fatal to humans, especially small humans with only partially developed immune systems. The rats had become a threat to my children, and I had to eliminate that threat. I put grain bait in the ceiling, and the strychnine wiped out the rodents quickly.

Everything was still for two days. No more grit of teeth on wood. Even the urine smell began to fade.

And then the smell of death was everywhere. That stench of rotting rat meat completely overpowered the urine smell. Within a few days, thousands of bloat flies cascaded out of those light fixtures, thudding into walls and windows. Fat things that buzzed in all directions, swarms of them. It took weeks to get rid of them. They'd die and another generation would replace them, dead flies piled over every surface in the garage. Dried out husks that crunched underfoot with every step we took.

Funny how it always works that way. We solve problems and create a series of new ones in the process.

But I would solve the biggest problem of them all here

soon. I'd kill the biggest rat of all. Or so I hoped.

I opened my eyes and blinked a few times, readying myself to stir the soup. Only then did I realize how sore my eyelids were, how tired I was, how clouded my thoughts were, my mind fogged up like the mirror in the bathroom after a long, hot shower.

I sat up, and that strain returned to my spine. The weight of the empty world.

Fiona

He lifted the spoon to his face, a droplet of soup hanging off the bottom where the rounded part narrowed into the handle. He hesitated a moment with it just shy of his lips, perhaps trying to avoid the soup giving way onto his chin or shirt. Cupping the opposite hand under the sloppy spoon, he finally landed the lentil sludge between his teeth. His lips closed around it, and he mushed it around in his mouth a moment and swallowed.

In my memory, it's like his lips filled my entire field of vision just then, like I was watching them on a huge iMAX screen in 3-D. This close up, the shapes lost their meaning. They became two flaps of fat covering his teeth hole. They looked all greased up with food, too, the shininess spreading to coat the pale flesh in the corners of his mouth.

Disgusting.

"Delicious, delicious soup," he said.

"Thank you."

He locked eyes with me and smiled, shaking his head a little. Then he went right back to shoveling heaping scoops of poison into his mouth. It was almost weird how easy it was. Almost disturbing.

I remembered that the rats were trickier. They were smarter. They didn't gorge themselves on the poison right away. They tested it, some evolutionary leap based on their inability to vomit. We had to put un-poisoned grain up there first for a few days to train them that this type of food from this location was OK and they could go all-you-can-eat-buffet nuts on it. Then, and only then, can you drop the strychnine hammer of death on them. By that time, some of the rats are so greedy that they will eat enough poison to kill 20. Quite a change from that first day when none of them would eat enough to matter.

Anyway, Doyle had no such evolutionary trait to assist him. No built in cautiousness. He just spooned the goop straight down his gullet as fast as he could.

I snapped back to the moment when I realized he was looking at me, his eyebrows raised like he'd just asked a question, though I don't think he had.

I swirled my spoon in my soup and pretended to eat some. I had set aside some for myself, of course, sans strychnine. Watching his mouth had killed any shred of appetite I'd had, though.

Doyle raised a fist to his mouth just then, his balled up hand blocking my view of those lips, a curious gesture that he held for a long, awkward moment.

Dear Jesus! Could it be taking effect so quickly? It seemed too fast. But then… maybe. I held my breath and watched, waiting for convulsions, for spasms and hacking and projectile vomiting.

Instead he cleared his throat and spoke.

"I've been thinking about what you talked about."

I had to concentrate to speak, picturing my tongue moving and my jaw working up and down before either of them would comply.

"What's that?"

"About finding a group. You're right, you know? We have to do that. We have to put every effort into finding others. It scares me, but what use is a life when it's lived like this? Alone in our cells. Confused and afraid and closed off from the world. We have to take that leap of faith. Believe that we can find someone worth trusting and make a real go of it."

I smiled a little. Nodded. He went on.

"I don't know if you noticed, but I've been keeping to myself these past few days, trying to wrap my head around all of it, trying to find a way to make it all make sense. And I realized that my faith in humanity could outweigh my fear of it. Not only that it could, but that it must, or all is already lost."

I watched another spoonful of strychnine breach his lips, his tongue flicking out to collect a little that had stuck to his top lip. I wanted to slap the utensil out of his hand, wanted to knock his bowl to the floor and dump the soup down the drain. But I sat, and I stared, and the wind rustled in and out of me like dead leaves scraping along a sidewalk.

I knew it was already too late.

Marissa

Hialeah, Florida
88 days before

My therapist told me to write down everything that happened like I was reliving it in a letter to someone I'd never met, focusing on communicating how I felt in each moment. Whatever that's supposed to accomplish. She has a bunch of fancy diplomas on her wall, however, so I feel obligated to play along. Here goes:

I chugged coffee at the stoplight, washing down half chewed chunks of Egg McMuffin with pitch black brew that scalded all the way down. This was supposed to be my break, a 55 minute lunch to split the twelve hour shift at the hospital into manageable pieces. Instead I was forcing down fast food and weaving around the slow-ass drivers to get home as fast as possible.

The babysitter had left a message that my 8-year-old son, Tony, was sick. Really sick, Candice said, and I needed to come home. Fine. Whatever. I'll take a break from caring for sick people in the hospital by driving home to care for another one.

How I felt in this moment: Annoyed. Candice had pulled this crap before. She was a worrier, only seventeen, kind of paranoid and gullible at the same time. She clutched a pillow to her chest while she watched all of those shows where fake ghost experts pretended to investigate haunted houses and crap. Utter garbage.

But what was I going to do? I had to check on my son. Just in case Candice wasn't crying wolf for once. I couldn't risk it.

After the last morsel of McMuffin slid down my esophagus, my hands fumbled in my purse on autopilot, retrieving and lighting the cigarette before I even realized what they were playing at. That's the funny thing about nurses. Despite working in hospitals around droves of people with cancer and emphysema, many of us smoke. Maybe most of us. I couldn't tell you why. Something about a nicotine break makes me feel like I'm getting away from the bullshit when almost nothing else does, I guess. Maybe it's like that for all of the others, too.

I cracked the window, eyes flicking from the road to watch the smoke trailing off the tip of my Winston drift through the opening and disappear. My jaw clenched and unclenched over and over. It tends to do that when I'm pissed off.

I arrived at our condo, parked, stubbed out my cig in the ashtray, and headed for the back door. I cut a corner through the grass, hopping over the little shrub that separated the yard from the sidewalk. The plant snagged the ankle of my scrubs and just about knocked me over. I think if I had gone down, I would have ripped it out of the ground on the spot.

I tried the door, found it locked. Typical Candice. I banged a fist on the steel and started digging for my keys.

The door inched open, fearful blue eyes shining in the sliver of a gap for a beat before it opened the rest of the way. I brushed past her on the way in, my feet thumping on the linoleum as I rounded the island in the kitchen and moved toward the stairs.

"Is he in his room?"

She didn't answer, just blinked several times.

"Hello! Is Tony in his room?"

"On the couch."

I changed directions to head that way. All of the curtains were drawn in the living room, so it felt like walking into a basement or into the shade of the woods.

Tony lay on his back, staring at the ceiling, eyes glazed. A fuzzy green blanket bunched around his chin like a scarf, making it look like he was just a head lying there on a throw pillow. Black and purple surrounded his eyes, the flesh there the shade of an eggplant and puffy looking. His breathing sounded a little raspy, too. Perhaps slower than usual.

"How you feeling, baby?"

His eyes shifted to look at me, and he blinked a few times, but he didn't say anything. His expression remained blank. I fell into nursing mode almost instantly, charting the assessment in my head. *Patient is not alert or oriented but is responding to normal verbal.*

How I felt in this moment: Concerned. Almost embarrassed that I'd been so mad at Candice when my boy looked quite sick after all.

The babysitter slunk into the room behind me and moved to the other side of the couch, her fist tightened and pressed into her lips as she looked down on Tony.

"Has he not been responding like this?" I asked.

Candice shook her head. No, he's not been responding? Or no, this is a new phenomenon? I didn't even bother asking her.

I knelt next to him, fishing a hand into the blanket to check his pulse. The seconds ticked away on my watch while I counted. After thirty seconds, I multiplied the number by two. 108 beats per minute. A little elevated but still technically within the normal range for his age. His skin felt cool and damp, though. Not sweaty, exactly. Almost more like touching the flesh of an amphibious creature.

"He was burning up earlier," Candice said, her voice wavering a little. "Now he's chilly so I got him wrapped up in that blanket. I didn't really know what to do, so…"

I nodded.

"You did good, Candice. I'm glad you called me. Has he thrown up at all or had loose stools?"

"No. Wait. You mean, like, diarrhea?"

"Yes."

"No. I mean, I don't think so. I didn't check that out or anything."

She put that fist against her lips again.

I looked down at Tony, and his eyes locked with mine, eyelids squeezing closed in slow motion flurries that somehow reminded me of an intelligent cat. His breath caught on mucus gathered in the back of the throat and scratched in and out. That happened often in the hospital with bed-ridden patients, especially those right at the end. The noise bothered the families, but it wasn't actually a big deal. Totally normal and manageable. Sounded worse than it was.

I rubbed his chest through the blanket, feeling the rise and fall of his ribcage.

"Does your stomach hurt, baby?"

Tony just looked at me, slow blinking some more. I couldn't get a great look at him in this gloomy room.

"Open the curtains, would you?"

Candice obliged, and gray light poured through the glass. That's when I realized how pale he was. His skin shone the color of cream apart from the bruised looking eyes.

"We'll take him in," I said. "I'll call and arrange things."

Candice's lip quivered.

"Is he... Will he...?"

"He'll be fine, Candice. Here. Take my keys and clear the clutter out of my backseat so he can lay back there. You can just throw all of the papers and stuff on the floor."

In this moment I felt: Hm... I want to say cautiously optimistic. I was glad to be here to take care of this. Tony looked pretty bad off, but we were handling things.

Just as I handed Candice the keys, however, Tony sat up, bolting upright like a deranged killer in a horror movie who had been presumed dead. He looked at me, eyes wild and wide, mouth agape.

He leaned forward and vomited blood. It pooled before him, thick red streams cascading over the puffy green blanket and drizzling to the floor.

Fiona

Beckley, West Virginia

138 days later

Doyle rested on the love seat in front of the window, and the gray drained the light out of the day behind him. A hand rested on his gut, fingers wriggling.

"Guess it's been too long since I had a finely cooked meal like that. My digestive system doesn't know what to do with good food anymore."

Sweat beaded on his forehead, and he grimaced a little. God, I wished it could just be over already. I wanted to run out of there, just rush out into the woods and belly flop in the snow and disappear. Bury myself. Fill my mouth up full of white powder to take my breath away.

But no. No, I would stay. I would offer him what comfort I could. I would make sure he didn't die alone.

"You want a glass of water?" I said.

"That'd be great."

I went to the backroom and ladled some water for him. A little splashed down and wet my fingers. I noticed then that the two big chapped lines crisscrossed on the back of my hand had scabbed over. It looked almost like a black X in the shade back here, the size of a quarter. Something about it made me shudder.

I walked back out and handed over the beverage. He guzzled the water, one hand still cradling his belly. He chugged most all of it down in one gulp, gasping when he finally came up for air, speaking bursts of words in those spaces between breaths.

"Thanks. My throat tightened up on me something fierce. Like a pain from my stomach all the way to the back of my mouth. Constricted feeling. Never felt anything like it before."

"I can get you a piece of ginger candy. That stuff is magic. Always helps calm my stomach."

His eyebrows crinkled up as he considered the idea.

"Yeah, sure. If you think it might help."

I went to the kitchen and fished one out of a tin for him.

"You're lucky. I bought these in bulk back in the day. Still have a bunch."

"I don't feel too lucky just now."

He paused for a beat and went on.

"Sorry. I'm not trying to be rude about the soup or anything. I know it's not your fault. Just… I'm in some serious pain is all."

"No need to apologize, Doyle. I just wish you weren't hurting."

He nodded and stuck the candy in his mouth. It clicked against his teeth as he adjusted it.

"Do you chew these?"

"No. You suck on them. Or I do, anyhow. They get stuck in my teeth if I chew on 'em."

He nodded again.

Things got quiet for a long moment. I folded my arms, watching him out of the corner of my eye from the other side of the room. It couldn't be long now, could it?

"Come sit with me. If you want."

"Oh, sure. I was just trying to think if there's anything else I could do to help you."

My legs felt heavy, limp, almost dead. I knew I must be in shock or getting there.

I plopped down in the seat next to him, the couch cushions cold against my back, the upholstery a little rough, a little worn. We looked into each other's eyes, and he shook his head and grimaced some more.

I turned my head and looked out at the room, that urge to flee coming over me again. The sound of my heartbeat seemed to swell up and up in volume until it was the loudest thing. The only thing. Not racing, really. Just a steady thump like a kick drum pounding out an even beat. A knocking vibration that only I could hear. Through that noise, this feeling came over me like I was missing something, like I was forgetting something important.

He was talking then, his lips moving, but I couldn't hear his words. Couldn't hear anything but my pulse, my blood, that thumping ball of muscle in my chest.

The idea was there then, the thing I was missing. It flitted just on the edge of things still, but I could feel it arriving, could sense it gurgling up from my subconscious thoughts to emerge in my conscious mind like I was reeling it in on a fishing line.

This was it. It was here:

What if Doyle was fucking with me?

Marissa

Hialeah, Florida
88 days before

I handled the car with aggression, putting all of my weight on the accelerator and jerking in and out of lanes to weave around the slow asses. Candice huffed and puffed in the passenger seat next to me, a white knuckled grip on the door handle, tears in her eyes.

Tony lay in the back with blood smeared down his face. He actually felt a little warmer after vomiting, his face, at least, though I wasn't sure if that was a good thing or a bad thing. His breathing was loud as hell still. He blinked up at the ceiling, not terribly concerned from what I could tell. I thought he could be in shock.

How I felt in this moment: Determined. I didn't let the fear in, didn't let it touch me. I didn't even think about what might be wrong with him. He was going to be fine. That's all there was to it.

I flicked my arms to the left and the car flitted into oncoming traffic to make it around vehicles stopped at an intersection. I ground the heel of my hand into the horn as we zoomed through the red light.

"I'm sorry to ask this," Candice said. "But do you think… I mean… could it be Ebola? Because we've touched… we're both… his blood."

She held up her bloody hands, turning them back and

85

forth like she was displaying a nice pair of gloves in a commercial. Red ran up to my wrists as well. I focused so as to not scream at her.

"If it's Ebola or something similarly contagious, we've been exposed, but we're driving straight to the hospital, aren't we? What else would you suggest we do at this point, Candice?"

"Nuh-nothing. I don't know."

Tony groaned in the backseat.

"Are you OK, baby?" I said.

No response. Just raspy breathing, and then a wet sound. Gushing is the best word I can think of for it.

I turned to Candice, who looked into the backseat to check on him.

"Is he OK?"

She studied him a moment, eyes squinted.

"No. I don't think so. He just… crapped a bunch of blood, I think. It's soaking through his blankets, getting all over."

I slapped her then. My hand was open, but I delivered the blow with some force. Not one of those girly slaps that connects with a high pitched clap. This was a solid thud. It snapped her head around, and her cheeks went all red.

I don't know why I did it. I guess I didn't like the way she worded what she said, but I don't think she was thinking very clearly.

Tony was going to make it, of course. I wasn't going to let her suggest otherwise.

Candice faced away from me, shoulders angled toward the window as we flew past a cluster of mini-vans. Only nine blocks now. The rasp still grated in and out behind me, so I knew Tony was hanging on back there.

I heard the moan of the siren before the twirling red and blue lights caught my eye in the mirror. The police. About five cars back and looking poised to close the gap.

"Shit," Candice said next to me. "We can't stop now. He won't make it."

She locked eyes with me, brushed the tousled hair out of her face. Her cheeks still shone red, but there was a fierce look in the set of her brow now. A defiant look.

"I know," I said. "We aren't stopping, baby. Not a fucking chance."

Despite everything going on, I couldn't help but smile just a little, and Candice returned an evil grin my way. I was impressed that she had gotten over the slap so quickly, and I was glad for it. I guess the new threat kind of rallied us back together. For Tony's sake.

We snaked around traffic, slaloming into the opposite lane when necessary. The cop car matched our every move, gaining on us. Three cars back, then two cars back.

The siren's warble intensified as the cop car closed to within a car length of us, a piercing wail that shifted and kicked into a faster paced whoop once the car was right on top of us, close enough for bumper to bumper contact. The volume surrounded and overwhelmed me, eliciting a physical response. A tingle throbbed in my chest and clambered up into my throat as the siren gargled out choppy sounds.

I gritted my teeth, watching the lights spin in the rearview mirror, watching the cop's expressionless face through the windshield. Some small part of me wanted to stop, to pull over and give up just to make the shrill screeching go away.

My fingers fumbled along the arm rest, finding the window button and pressing it. The sheet of glass descended into its crevasse, and I stuck my arm out the window, waving the cop up beside us.

"Come on, assfuck. Get up here."

An almost imperceptible shift of the eyebrows in the rearview told me that the officer had registered my intent. His car jerked a little, showed some flash of hesitation before he approached.

He didn't pull alongside us, however. Opted to tailgate us pretty good instead.

Total douche.

Fine by me. We could use his siren to clear a path all the way to the hospital.

Fiona

My eyes snapped to that bandaged spot on the back of his right hand. Clean white gauze still occupied that square of his flesh, held down by a perimeter of medical tape. The mark. The mark of the beast. Could it still be real? Could this demon be torturing me? Making me feel guilty when he knows I shouldn't?

I squinted, as though I could look through the man, as though I could hold my eyes just right and see through his skin, see what was really going on in there.

The notion that I was mistaken or morbid or insane still lingered, but I couldn't know, could I? I couldn't say with any certainty.

He looked at me then, and his pupils had swollen into black pits, exaggerated and demonic and strange. This expression on his face seemed to convey equal parts fright and stimulation. Were these symptoms of the poison? Or was he morphing into his ultimate form in front of me?

"Something isn't right," he said.

He spoke between clenched teeth, and though his eyes still met mine, his neck tilted at an odd angle so it almost seemed like he was talking to the ceiling instead of me.

"I'm cramping up. All of me. All of my muscles."

His feet curled under him, toes and ankles flexing so it

almost looked like he was attempting to do the pointe technique in ballet, trying to stand up on his tiptoes.

He fought against it, wriggling on the couch, strained noises torn from his throat and delivered through his clenched mouth. The muscles of his face tightened as he squirmed, eyebrows raising first, then his cheeks going taut, his lips pulling back to expose his teeth in a fixed, demented grin. It looked like when a dog's lip gets caught in a way that exposes its front teeth, something off in the expression it created. Something a little dim and unintentional.

To my surprise, he stood. His hands rubbed at his chest and his shoulders a moment, and then he walked to the other side of the living room. Jerky footsteps pounded on the floor and made the glass stand in the corner shake. It sounded like cutlery shaking around in a drawer pulled open too fast, all the forks and knives and spoons rattling against each other.

He hesitated in the threshold between the living room and kitchen, his hands still feeling up and down his person. Spastic energy radiated from each of his movements, every step and gesture somehow twitchy, flickering, nervous looking.

He turned back to look at me, those pools of black staring into my eyes like a wounded animal's. His mouth still wore that dopey grin, but his eyes conveyed fright and injury and defeat all at once. Panic. And it struck me what a wretched creature a human could be, what loathsome, ugly beings we are, though I didn't know if I thought this because of him or because of myself. Maybe it was both of us.

His neck jerked, muscles convulsing, angling his head up toward the ceiling again. The muscle spasm turned his eyes away from mine and seemed to lock his head in place, chin jutting skyward. His eyes blinked a few times and swiveled within his motionless head so he looked like one of those creepy glass-eyed dolls.

We made eye contact again, and he spoke through clenched teeth, his lips just faintly moving at all.

"EpiPen."

"What?"

"I must be having some kind of allergic reaction! Do you have an EpiPen?"

"I'm not... Just... Let me look."

I rose and strode past him to the bathroom, legs jiggling beneath me like Jello. The shade grew stronger as I approached this part of the house, the little light slanting in from the hallway not helping me much, and my eyes wouldn't get time to adjust. My fingers scrabbled along the cabinet door, struggling for a moment to find the knob. I opened it, the intertwined smells of soap and toothpaste greeting me. I could just make out the lighter rectangular shape within that I knew to be the first aid kit. I grabbed it and walked back to the living room.

He still stood there in the same spot, fidgeting fingers picking at the seam at the bottom of his shirt. That unintentional smile seemed to have gained intensity. His lips pulled so taut that they flipped open a little along the edges like they were about to flip inside out, and those creases under his cheeks deepened to match them. His breathing took on a labored hiss, little flecks of spit throbbing between his teeth with each breath.

Back in the light, I crouched and ripped open the first aid

kit. I moved with urgency as though this might actually help him. My fingers picked and poked through alcohol and gauze tape and little pill bottles and utensils until I found the cylinder marked epinephrine auto-injector.

"Here."

I handed it over and he popped the blue safety lid off. He held the tip of it just shy of his neck and paused.

"Neck, right?"

"What?"

"Do I jam this into my neck or what?"

"I don't know. I thought you did it in your leg."

An angry sigh whistled between his teeth, and he turned the pen sideways to read the fine print on it. Those demon pupils stared at the pen, his eyes going crossed and uncrossed in little twitches. He leaned into the candlelight, slowly bringing the cylinder close enough to almost touch the tip of his nose, and after a beat tried moving it farther out, almost arm's length.

"I can't."

He tossed the pen to me, and I wasn't ready for it, so it ricocheted off my arm and skittered across the floor into the kitchen.

"What do you mean, you can't?"

"I can't read the fucking thing! It's all blurry and shit."

I stooped to pick up the EpiPen and brought it close to read those tiny letters.

"It says to place the black tip against the fleshy portion of your outer thigh. You may give the injection directly through your clothing."

He poised his right hand near his thigh, curling his fingers

92

as though they held the pen. My eyes flitted to that bandaged spot on the back of his hand for a beat before they flicked back to skim to the next pertinent bit of instruction.

"'With a quick motion, push the auto-injector firmly against your thigh. This will release the spring-loaded needle that injects the dose of EpiPen. Hold the auto-injector in place for a few seconds after activation.'"

I looked up at him.

"That's pretty much it."

I tossed the pen, which he caught and injected in one motion. It snicked as it met his thigh, and he held it there, a strange projectile tube with its head smothered in the leg of his jeans.

I hated to see him, to gaze upon him, to know the havoc I'd wreaked. The look on his face was so demented, like some awful subhuman beast in an old monster movie.

But it would all be over soon, I thought.

Fiona

It wasn't over soon. At all. It went on for hours. His body contorted, head, neck, and back arching, all of the muscles of his torso turned to cords, to pieces of rope that pulled him as hard as they could, tried their best to bend his spine the wrong way. In time, his legs stiffened as well and stuck straight out like tree branches, his toes still curling in on themselves.

We sat on the love seat. I held his hand and rubbed his chest with my other hand. I didn't know what else to do. A fevered feeling settled upon me, a heat that somehow detached me from this moment. I talked to him, said soothing words, caring words, like a nurse, like a mother, but most of me was somewhere else, somewhere far away.

He made noises, but he hadn't spoken actual words in a while now. I didn't think he could speak with the way the muscles of his face had twisted up. He looked more like a Halloween mask than a man by this time, like some gruesome special effects makeup. Something designed to frighten small children, to spoil their dreams.

"You'll be OK," I said. "Just try to stay calm, baby. You're having some kind of seizure, but it will pass if you keep calm."

He moaned a little, drool spilling out of one side of his mouth. The fear was evident in his face even with the skin

94

pulled so tight that he barely looked human.

His eyes looked to be all pupil now. The blackest, deadest holes like those of a shark, I'd say, if he didn't look so scared.

Something about the way he stiffened made it seem like he was turning to wood, muscles hardening into fibrous, grained lumber. He tried to thrash against it, tried to stave off the growing rigidity with flailing and stretching and squirming, but his range of motion tightened and tightened until the best he could muster was the faintest quiver.

Pulling on his arm really did feel like pulling a tree limb. It was hard, but not entirely inflexible like steel. It had that little give to it, like pulling a maple branch and letting it snap back.

And I rubbed his chest some more, and I told him that he would be OK, but I knew he wouldn't. He would never be OK.

His body trembled, my hand vibrating where it rested on his sternum. His breathing was uneven now, and soon those neural pathways from his brain to his lungs would get crushed by these rigid muscles to the point that his respiration cut off. He would die here, contorted, paralyzed, unable to breathe and fully conscious all the while, just like the rats up above the ceiling in the garage.

And all I could do now was hold my palm to his chest and feel his body shake, a haphazard tremor that seemed to convey great force. I hoped that it offered him some comfort, at least.

Time passed. I don't know how long. I zoned out for a while, staring off at nothing until his breathing changed.

Breaths jerked in and out of him in uneven bursts, sometimes cutting out for a good 20 seconds or more before resuming. His back and neck arched as far as they would go, curling his body closer and closer to the shape of a capital letter C. The angles of everything made it look that much more grotesque, like something you might find at the scene of car crash.

His chin tucked into the top of his collar bone and just kept inching back until it was like his head was almost behind him, almost under him, too, in fact, as his pelvis arched up above the rest of him. His arms bent up against his torso, muscles all knotted up.

The breathing cut out again and stayed out, stayed silent. I heard one little throat noise. A click. That was all the effort he could muster.

His body shook more violently, chest quaking for what felt like a long time but was probably only a minute or so. He looked like a stretched out spring about to break.

And then the motions cut off, and he was still. He was dead.

Marissa

Hialeah, Florida
88 days before

The traffic parted before us like the Red Sea. The siren screamed and everyone got the eff out of the way, cars and trucks and vans drifting off to the sides. It was a good feeling.

We roared the final blocks to the hospital in a dead straight line like a dragster at top speed, and my blood thrummed in my ears, and pins and needles throbbed in my hands. I could barely hear Tony's breath over the engine, but it was there, so I knew he would make it.

The hospital took shape to our left, a towering brick building with ornate spires that made it look like a handful of churches stuck together rather than a medical building. I drove there most every day and never looked at it, but now I was, and it was immense and impressive. Regal, maybe. It sat back from the road, a grass field and a large parking lot lying between us and the front doors. Walls of stone the size of bowling balls surrounded both, piling up into gates around the driveway.

My eyes flicked to the rearview. Saw the policeman's body language shift in his seat, a sense of urgency now present in the carriage of his upper body. He seemed to get what was happening finally.

The cop car jutted through the gates and into the lot, pulling in front of us now, the siren's wail seeming to elongate as it changed directions and moved away from us. I followed a beat behind, and we zoomed to the front of the building, flying past the grass and the cars, the red and blue lights twirling over all of it.

My heart shimmied up into my neck as we wound around the curved drive to the front doors. Everything in my throat squeezed, and blood flowed all through me, squishing a fevered, red feeling up into my face. Something like standing too long in direct sunlight and growing dizzy.

Time seemed fast and slow at the same time. The cop car jerked to a stop, and the officer ran inside for help. Candice and I released our seatbelts and got out in unison, opening up the back doors and pulling a limp Tony free. I grabbed his ankles and pulled while she lifted his shoulders, the bloody blankets falling away to reveal a scrawny pale boy gone purple around the eyes, his neck limp, his mouth dangling open. I saw him blink once, or I might have thought we were too late.

When we turned around, the cop was already there with nurses and a stretcher, and they grabbed my boy and flipped him onto the gurney, his arms and legs flopping like noodles. Candice and I stood shoulder to shoulder as we passed him off. The people must have been chattering and yelling around us, but I heard none of these things. I heard my pulse in my ears, that beat and swish of the blood flowing through me.

I stood and watched them wheel him away, watched the automatic doors open like a mouth to swallow him up, watched them disappear, the door closing behind them.

The pins and needles in my hands crawled up my arms and swelled in my chest.

We made it. We actually made it.

Fiona

Beckley, West Virginia
138 days after

I dragged the body out into the snow, as stiff as a statue. He was heavy, a load to move, but in some way I thought his stiffness might have been making him easier to maneuver than a limp corpse would have been.

Burying him wasn't really an option with the snow and the ground probably frozen, but I got him out into the edge of the woods. That felt like he wasn't completely exposed, completely left out in the open, at least, I thought.

I stood over the corpse, the arched body face down in the white, the hair ruffled on the back of his head. It seemed like something should happen, something dramatic, something emotional, but nothing did. I'd waited all that time that I sat with Doyle, I knew, for my feelings to bubble up from my subconscious, waited for the involuntary reaction to occur so I would know how to feel about it all, but nothing ever came. I remained numb, listless, shocked.

I realized that the strychnine didn't feel like something I did, something I caused. It just felt like something that happened. Something that was over now. Some fact of the universe to be merely observed, not judged.

I walked back to the house, following that weird, uneven trail in the snow where I'd dragged the curled up body. I looked out over the emptiness in the distance, the stark landscape, the untouched snow in all directions for as far as I could see. The wind howled, and the powder kicked up everywhere, sheets of it moving in diagonal lines in the air around me. It was so quiet just then, and somehow it seemed colder than ever, lonelier than ever.

So maybe I didn't cry. Maybe I didn't scream, didn't wail, didn't throw a tantrum.

But the world sure seemed quieter now, and it sure seemed empty as hell.

As soon as I made it back inside, I went to work on the fire, building it up and up, a teepee of split logs nestling over flaming balls of phone book paper. The orange brightened when the wood caught. The warmth grew and grew until the heat surrounded me, seeming to compress my ribcage, to press itself deeper and deeper into the flesh of my face, so hot I could imagine blisters forming on my cheeks and lips, my skin frothing up like spit bubbles. I could even see the shimmer of heat distortion in the air around the stove, every line becoming a squiggle.

I didn't mind the heat, though. I wanted it. I wanted physical sensations strong enough to make me forget. It just made sense to me in that moment. Forget all of this and feel the warm surrounding me, enveloping me, swallowing me away from the empty world for a while.

All of the chapped places ached from my time out in the cold with the body. My lips stung, the cracks probably bleeding again. My hands hurt worst of all, though. I held them up, examined the way the lines on my palms had gone white and crusty. I balled my fingers up into fists and released a few times, watching those cracked lines in my hand crease and wrinkle like the edge of a sheet of paper.

And then I turned them over. The left hand looked normal, all things considered. Areas of my skin flaked here and there and one spot went a little pink and scabby, the irritated flesh pocked with tiny red spots.

A black wound marred my right hand, though. A matte black X that looked wrong entirely, more like ash than any skin or scab I'd ever seen, like the burned out coals left at the bottom of the stove. I squinted, trying to see the wound better. I felt as though I couldn't quite focus on it, couldn't quite see it correctly, but narrowing my eyes didn't seem to help at all.

I lowered my hand, the black mark drifting out of my view, and I stared into the fire. Just forget it. Forget all of it.

The flames curled around the wedges of wood, hugging them with orange arms. I focused on the flicker, on the heat once more biting at my face.

I closed my eyes, the warmth gripping my eyelids right away, and I could still sense the fire's glow fading and swelling in the stove. I let my mind drift, totally blank. In a way it felt like standing under the shower, the hot water soothing me, the heat in the air in a cloud around me, the atmosphere almost thick with warm.

Fiona

Beckley, West Virginia
139 days after

I dreamed of Doyle, of me on top of him, our hearts
thudding, our bodies moist with sweat, my skin against his.
The dark did not shroud him this time, though, did not cast
shadows that reduced him to a masculine silhouette. I saw
him as he was. As flesh and blood. As a stubbled jaw and wet
eyes. As a man.

He moved strangely, though. A fluidity marked his
movements, a liquid quality to the squirm of his chest and
shoulders and neck. But the heat filled my face and melted
such thoughts from my brain.

And I leaned back to tower over him again, to feel that
power once more. And I felt the chill where the air touched
my skin as our torsos parted, felt his eyes on my body, his
hands on my body. My eyelids narrowed to slits and then
closed, and I felt him writhing under me, slithering even,
something serpentine in his motions.

When I opened my eyes, the light in the room had
changed, going yellow. Bars of glow shined through the
shades, striping his face in light and dark, half blocking him
out. He licked his lips, tongue flicking in and out of the
shadows.

I brought my hands up to block him the rest of the way
out, palms sliding over the rough of his five o'clock shadow,

over the sweat slicked cheeks, fingers settling on the clammy skin of his eyelids. The hard bridge of his nose pressed into those meaty balls of muscle near my thumbs like a bird's beak.

He bucked his hips a few times, his pelvis thrusting as though to throw me off. I pressed harder on his face, thumbs seeming to disappear into those smile line folds along his nostrils. His torso wriggled, squirmed, and now he almost seemed more wormlike than snakelike, a slimy cylinder of thrashing flesh gripped between my thighs.

And finally he bucked and just stayed up in that upright position, all rigid, pelvis arched above the rest of him, and then I saw those shark black pupils peering out at me between my fingers, and the permanent smile etched onto the mouth below the heels of my hands.

I pulled back my hands, unveiling the scrunched up Halloween mask of a face, and then he grabbed me, one curled up arm unfurling, the hand latching onto my forearm and pulling me close. My face hovered just above that demented smile, close enough to see that his teeth had dried out from being exposed for so long. They looked like hunks of glossless porcelain.

I yanked my arm against the clasp of his fingers, but he was too strong. His hands had stiffened to the point that they no longer felt like human flesh against my skin but something solid and dense and inflexible.

I stopped fighting and looked upon him. My chest heaved, but his did not. He didn't move at all now except for those black nothing eyeballs swiveling to stay latched onto me.

I tried to jerk away one more time, and he pulled me closer still, and those dried out teeth opened up in slow

103

motion until his maw gaped before me, a ropey string of saliva stretching between his tongue and the roof of his mouth. Then I woke up.

Fiona

Beckley, West Virginia
140 days after

I still shudder when I remember the dream. Something about the series of images almost disturbs me more than actually witnessing Doyle's death, but I've had no nightmares since then. No dreams at all that I've recalled.

I'm burning through my wood faster than ever, but all I want to do is sleep and stare into the fire and forget it all. Forget who I am and all I've done.

Whenever I lose focus, my gaze drifts to those blackened lines on the back of my hand. My eyes fix themselves upon the X like it's an opening and they'll see something through the cracks. Something important.

The snow piles at the doors again. The flurries come off and on to stack more white on the ground, and the wind whips it around like it always does, sheets undulating and billowing in the air like white capes. I don't think we've had this much accumulation before Christmas in years. Maybe ever. And it's all for me, I guess.

I realize now that Doyle wasn't the antichrist. He couldn't be.

Because I am.

The black on my hand is my mark finally coming clear to me, revealing my core truth. The poisoning all but proves it, doesn't it?

Even after all that's come to pass, all the warnings I'd been given, I had my choice, my final chance to trust humanity, to trust Doyle, and I threw it away. I killed an innocent being, a man who had done nothing but help me.

I'm not human. Not all the way. Some piece is missing. I can see that in a way, see how it was always so, see how I chose the path to cement it.

I beg God to forgive me, but I know he can't.

Marissa

Hialeah, Florida
88 days before

Candice and I stood in the waiting area, hospital workers bustling around us. I'd called my supervisor somewhere in there to tell him I was dealing with an emergency, though I don't actually remember talking to him. It was a huge building, and we were several floors from where I worked. So strange to feel like foreigner, like a tourist in the same building in which I spent the bulk of my waking time.

A game show flashed on the TV, a screaming girl trying to win a Hyundai Sonata, but I couldn't pay attention, couldn't even sit down without the jitters creeping into my legs and standing me back up involuntarily. So I stood, and I shifted my weight from foot to foot to satisfy that restless part of me that couldn't keep still.

A man in the waiting area with a white mustache flecked with black watched us, his eyes just barely visible through the glare on his glasses. Maybe I was just paranoid, but it felt like the other people waiting in this area were staring at us, too.

I went to drum my fingers against my lips, another restless habit, I guess, but I stopped my hand just shy of making contact, remembering all of the blood just in time. Maybe that's why they were staring. I leaned over to Candice and whispered.

"Maybe we should wash up."

She looked down at her hands, nodded.

We walked around the corner to the ladies' room. The light was different in there, brighter and harsher, reflecting off of glossy tiles the off-white shade of a smoker's teeth. The fluorescent bulbs buzzed above us as well, fizzy sounds like insects. I stood in front of the sink and watched the pink swirl off of my hands and spiral down the drain, the warm water something of a shock on my icy hands. It prickled at first, but then it felt good.

I left them under the water even after the pink swirls were gone. I let my consciousness filter down to just the feeling of that warmth in my fingers, as much as I could, anyway. My eyes went half out of focus so every edge softened and smeared into everything else. My mind wandered over the thought that the temperature in human hands drops rapidly when adrenaline enters the bloodstream, that this was surely why my hands were so cold.

A man's throat cleared behind me, and my vision's focus sharpened. I turned, the sound of the water slapping the porcelain ringing out behind me.

I didn't think much of it at first that the doctor standing there was wearing a mask, and I didn't realize until later that he was keeping his distance on purpose, hovering in the doorway to the ladies' room. He locked eyes with me, and I waited for him to say something, anything, to expound upon Tony's condition, to give some clue as to what we were dealing with. Instead he jerked a thumb at Candice and me, and a group of people in Hazmat suits filed into the restroom to grab us.

I held his gaze, though, even as the gloved hands closed

around my triceps and latched onto that flap of flesh in each of my armpits.

"What about my son? Is he OK?"

I could see a puff of breath ripple along the surface of his mask.

"The boy was dead by the time they wheeled him through the front door."

Fiona

Beckley, West Virginia
142 days after

I can't sleep anymore. I lie here and stare into the fire. There is nothing else left.

I will be out of wood in two days. Maybe three. I will not gather more. I will let go, let the cold do with me what it will.

I think the spot on my hand is growing, bigger and blacker. I wonder sometimes if it will spread over my skin like burn marks, the flesh cracking to reveal the molten orange of hell inside me, the magma coursing all through me.

I beg God to give me a sign, to give me any reason to carry on. I know it's too late, that I am a wretched thing beyond redemption, but I beg anyway because there's nothing else.

What if this is hell? What if hell is an eternity alone in an empty world? The place where you dwell on your mistakes, your flaws, forever.

Fiona

The heavens opened, and the rains poured down, fat droplets rapping at the windows and beating on the roof. When the wind blew, raindrops angled onto the porch, the water exploding on impact, spraying everywhere.

The temperature crept up and up, the snow shrinking away from the doors, the rain pummeling it, melting it one drop at a time. Steam rose off of the ground after a while, a fog that thickened like a wet blanket strung up in the air.

The downpour stretched on for hours and hours, swelling at times and waning at others but never stopping entirely. It was hard to believe that the snow pile could shrink so much. Within a day, oblong patches of the asphalt and concrete had become visible. It could all be gone as early as tomorrow. It had never melted that quickly before that I could remember.

I was glad, I realized, that none of my windows faced the woods. Where he lay, I mean. I could only imagine what the water and warmth would do to the corpse, the skin and muscle going pale gray and then liquefying and oozing away.

Anyway, I didn't take this mini-heat wave as a sign from God, exactly. Still, it would at least mean I wouldn't freeze to death when the wood ran out. Not right away, anyhow.

Fiona

Beckley, West Virginia
145 days after

It's gone. No more snow. The soggy grass lies flat, mashed to the ground by snow and rain and held down by the mud. A stream of runoff flows down the street still. I imagine the low lying areas toward town are flooded, though I have no plans to verify this theory.

I sit and look out at the flattened grass now mostly beige, and I feel a pinch, a pull, a desire to move toward some conclusion. What will I do if no sign from God comes soon? Before I assumed that I would freeze within a few days, but the change in weather seems to have granted me a little more time. I'm not sure how to use it. I'm never sure what anything means anymore.

Fiona

Beckley, West Virginia
147 days after

What if I'm just a sick animal? A creature shuffled into existence here by the random whims of evolution. Nothing more. An existence totally without inherent meaning, totally without purpose.

What if there's no antichrist? No God? What if it was all a lie that led me to this?

What if I just pulled apart from reality at some point? A broken brain. Not right in the head. Even before the poisoning, maybe.

The kind of person who wants to smother someone's face during sex? Sounds like something an ape would do, doesn't it? Like a lady praying mantis decapitating her mate. Sounds like an animal satisfying irrational impulses. Is that all there is? And what if those impulses are the normal part of me? The animal part of me that wants to survive and reproduce. Is that what the humanity in me is, with this consciousness serving as the intruder, the perversion? Certainly those impulses will carry on long after my stream of thoughts is extinguished. Whatever people that are left, they will eat and fight and fuck for as long as they can hang in there. They will serve those animal impulses until the end, while all of the individual selves die off, ultimately meaningless.

Maybe the animal part is humanity and all of the rest is

fluff, some high-minded delusion.

I look at the black X on my hand. Is it some supernatural symbol? Or is it just a dark scabbed up patch of human flesh from getting wet and chapped out in the cold that happens to look a little strange? Which is more reasonable? Which do I even want to believe?

Fiona

Beckley, West Virginia
150 days after

The cold returns, more bitter than before. More cruel. The winter cares not for the lives it takes, the baby mice and squirrels and raccoons that all go rigid by its hand. It thinks nothing of these things. It has no feelings. None at all.

Frost lines every window, a smudged layer of ice on the inside, fogging up my view. I press my hand against the pane of glass to clear an area to look through, frigid drops of water rolling down the lengths of my fingers. The rectangles I open re-frost within an hour or so, though. I don't think I'll bother anymore.

It must be below zero out there now, and it'll be that much worse after dark. It seems colder without the snow, like the layer of white provides a little insulation. A blanket laid out on the ground to keep it a little warm, at least. The soil that was soggy yesterday now looks dry and cracked, white layers of frost cover every blade of grass. The texture of the white almost looks like fur or fuzz or mold. I crunch through it on my way to the well, and the cold makes my nostrils sting and itch like crazy the second I step into it. I spat to test it, and my spittle froze upon hitting the cement stoop by the back door.

I'm down to my last two loads of wood, perhaps a few hours worth, and I can see my breath in here already, feel the sting of the cold in the tip of my nose.

I could walk to Doyle's, of course. He has a pile of wood, enough to get through the winter. I could either wheel some back here or just stay there.

But I won't do either of these things. I will stay the course here, wrap myself in blankets and see whether or not I survive the long, black night.

Marissa

I guess that's the end of the story, for the most part.

I sat in isolation for a couple of hours before anyone would talk to me. I knew based on the ventilation system in my room that they feared the worst. Some airborne Ebola-type nightmare.

I couldn't bring myself to turn on the TV or touch the bottle of water they'd left for me on the nightstand. I sat on the edge of the hospital bed, that groggy feeling coming over me again like standing under a too-hot shower. And I think I spent much of that time thinking that it was all a mistake, thinking that I wouldn't believe Tony was gone until I saw it for myself.

But when one of the doctors came by in a Hazmat suit and told me that Candice was sick, I knew it was real. It was all real. A couple of the nursing assistants that had wheeled Tony in were the next to fall ill, and the cop that helped us wasn't long after. I'm sure there were more that they didn't tell me about, maybe more that they didn't even know of.

All of these people died within 36 hours.

I'm still here, though I don't know why.

They let me out of quarantine after four days. I think they needed the room for someone who was actually sick by then. They told me the CDC would be in touch since I seem to be immune, but so far that has just involved a physical and all these mandatory meetings with a shrink. No real medical tests. Nothing that seems to matter. Classic government bullshit, right?

I never did see my boy again, either. They said his body was in quarantine at an undisclosed location for further study. The last time I saw him, strangers wheeled him away from me, and the hospital door swallowed him up.

So yeah. That's it, I think.

How I feel in this moment: Some things are for no one to know. Just me. Is that OK? Or does the doctor really need me to parse the loss of my child even further?

Fiona

Beckley, West Virginia
151 days after

The fire died just before dusk. I threw a few more balls of phone book paper in once the wood was down to glowing coals, watched them open like blooming flowers and burst into flames, but I figured it was a little pointless to burn paper just to keep that flicker of light going for a few more minutes. It produced very little heat, flaming out quickly. It was visually stimulating, sure, but it offered no real substance.

The orange faded to black, and the little cracks and pops slowed and then stopped. No more smoke twirled up the chimney. No more light shined in the mouth of the stove. Not even a glimmer. The heat coming off of the metal faded to lukewarm.

With the fire gone, I blew out the candles to let the dark close in. I don't know why. To get it over with, maybe.

Black obliged that wish, descending to vanquish the day. I watched through the window as the darkest shade swallowed up the gray, eliminating all light, outside and in. It was so much darker without that shimmery layer of snow like a giant mirror reflecting light everywhere.

The cold followed the dark's lead, though it came on slowly. The frost on the windows thickened, crystal shapes forming on the glass so it looked like a sheet of strange snowflakes growing there, or maybe like that frosty layer that forms on top of ice cream if it sits in the freezer too long.

I pulled the blankets up to my neck and let my head nestle back into my pillows. My face remained in the open, however, exposed. I needed, somehow, to stare into the dark, as pointless as that may seem. I did so, open eyes gazing up into nothing, blinking every once in a while just to remind myself that I was real.

I lied awake for what felt like a long time before the heaviness tugged at my eyelids. The temperature dropped in the room all the while. I could feel it on my ears and on the tip of my nose. I doubted it was even that late since the nights were so long now, but I wasn't sure.

Sleep settled upon me in time. Fitful sleep disturbed often by the cold. Not enough to draw me into a truly alert state, just a consistent disruption, a little shake that would pull me up to the surface, half-confused. I shivered all through the night, falling in and out of black dreams. The cold cinched around me, its grip crawling from my feet up into my legs and from my head down into the trunk of my body.

I woke up in the black, my hands and face mostly numb, my legs lacking feeling from the toe to halfway up the calf. My torso was more cool than cold, but it was getting there, little by little.

I fumbled in the dark for matches and lit a candle, a feat with numb fingers. It took more than a few tries. I had to trust the scrape of the match against the striking strip more than the feel, using my ears more than my hands or eyes.

And now I sit here in the candle's glow and write. The light flickers over the page, swelling and ebbing and changing its angle. The shadow from my pen shrinks and grows in unison with the flicker.

Steam coils from my mouth if I direct my head toward the glow of the candlelight, almost seeming to congeal in the air. I imagine my breath freezing into those frosty crystals from the window, and then I imagine those pointed ice formations trailing from my mouth down my throat and into my lungs, all of the wet places, the mucus membranes, frosted over just like the glass.

I pass my fingers over the candle's flame, venturing closer and closer without really feeling it. It only serves to wake the nerves up enough to sting from the cold. No real feelings. The candle still burns, but I think my glow is gone.

Fiona

Beckley, West Virginia
151 days after

My body shakes. My teeth chatter. My fingers and toes scream out, burning with cold. I took a few swigs of whiskey to soothe my head, to warm my throat and stomach with that alcohol burn. I know being drunk actually makes me more likely to freeze to death, more likely to forego shivering in my sleep and let the cold all the way in, but I couldn't resist. Even now, I sip at the bottle, barely containing the urge to chug it all down at once.

And still the night stretches on. No sign of daylight. No sign from God. No sign that anyone but me even exists.

I pile myself under blankets, but the warmth won't build. It won't take hold. I try to fidget, to move enough to create a little heat, but it's hard to keep going. I'm too tired.

I'm afraid that if I fall asleep again it will be the last time I do so. Even so, slumber is all I want.

Does this count as suicide? I think it must. I'm choosing this path, aren't I?

Another swig to wash that broth-like taste of acid reflux off of the back of my tongue. The sting feels good all the way down, a kind of warmth, a kind of subtle pain that cuts through the cold feelings, makes me forget my fingers and toes, makes me forget the way my body convulses.

I try to focus my thoughts in those post-drink moments,

122

to further consider that idea of me being the antichrist, or perhaps of Doyle being the antichrist, but it all blurs together in my head. Like my skull is a blender whirring all of my thoughts into a pasty puree, leaving me unable to discern anything but mush.

The windows offer me no light. No hope. And I wonder if the night will ever end. It doesn't seem possible. It seems like the darkness is infinite, the cold endless. It seems like the only things I will ever really know are the dark and the cold and myself. A candle and this pen and paper are the only weapons I have to fight it. Not great.

Maybe this really is hell. An endless night in an empty room, in an empty world, the cold claws of death tightening around me eternally.

Fiona

My eyes drifted closed a few times, the ambient sound filtering away into the silence of sleep. But I always shook myself awake, always lifted my chin, the sound of my breathing fading back into my consciousness.

When the first glimmer of gray encroached outside the windows, I was sure it was my imagination. I knew this night couldn't truly end. I knew my mind was playing tricks on me, conjuring hallucinatory images to comfort me.

The quiver in my torso rose and fell in a steady rhythm, a big shake that gave way to a smaller shake, that pattern repeating itself over and over. There was some comfort in the repetition. It seized my chest and squeezed as it rattled me, dictating the pattern of my respiration, requiring exhales to fall during the big shakes. I didn't mind its bossiness, though. I didn't mind much of anything anymore.

I realized that some lethargy must be falling over me, perhaps that listlessness that settles on people as hypothermia sets in, the slowing down that makes it possible to fall asleep and freeze to death peacefully. I couldn't say for sure, though. Maybe I was just tired due to the lack of sleep. Still, the pain in my hands and feet seemed smaller, my tolerance for my scenario seemed to be growing.

The sky went a few shades paler, some of the details in the

room fading back into view even through that layer of crusty frost on the windows. I could make out the white coffee mug on the TV stand next to the mattress, the curve of the handle taking shape if I squinted just right. This woke me up some, my heightened state of awareness turning the hurt back on in my fingers and toes like flipping a pain switch.

I'd made it through the night. That had to mean something.

I rose to my feet, stiff joints slow to obey, slow to bend as I'd commanded. My knees wobbled as my legs straightened up to bear my weight. My ankles popped one after the other as I forced them to flex. The constant muscle spasms and shivering made all of this more difficult, an extra variable in the balancing equation.

I bent at the waist, my upper body rocking atop my dead legs. I didn't force it. I just stood in that awkward position until things settled a little. Things evened out some in time, and I stood upright.

Leaving the blanket felt insane. Not that it was warm at this point, but it did shield my skin from the coldest, driest air, at least. It fell away as I stood, and the chill rushed in to press itself against me, worming through my pajamas to wrap itself around my body.

I wiped my nose and felt something hard and cold there. Strange. My fingers backtracked, retracing their steps to inspect further.

An actual piece of ice clung to the tip of my nose. Frozen snot. It formed a curved layer capping the end of my nose. I jammed the nails of my index finger and thumb under the edges of it and worked at it, ripping it free within a few seconds. To my fingers, it somehow felt like peeling apart a peanut M&M. To my nose, it was more like peeling off a hat that had adhered to my scalp and taking a thick layer of skin with it. The exposed dermis cried out when the cold touched it, an incredibly exposed feeling, like the chill was reaching inside of me now, rooting around beneath my skin.

I pinched my nose in the crook of my hand and held it there. It was equally cold, but it did keep the air away from the opened up place, protected the wound.

I walked across the room and back. My gait jerked a little, my joints loosening at uneven intervals, the inconsistencies making themselves felt in my footsteps. Still, it felt good to move, to walk. I knew I'd need to keep going, keep the muscles in my legs working to hold on to what little body heat I had left.

I paced back and forth endlessly, and the day took shape out the windows, the swirls of gray creeping in to combat the shadows around me. It still didn't quite feel real, perhaps because of the frost blocking up the windows like they'd been smeared with Crisco. I saw it in an abstract way, a general increase in light that occurred in slow motion, rather than witnessing firsthand the daylight falling upon the grass and the trees. Still, even the indirect way was heartening.

I rubbed my hands together as I walked to try to build up some warmth, tucking them back into my sleeves between rubs. The skin was so dried out that it felt like sliding together sheets of sandpaper. I'd strapped on my coat, feeling around in the dark by the back door to locate the coat rack. When there was enough light in here, I'd find my gloves and hat to cover myself a little better. Dumb to forgo them in the night, but I wasn't in my right state of mind. I knew that now.

Still, the walking had warmed me at least a little. The pain in my legs had shrunken back from my calves so it only really affected my feet now. That had to be a good sign.

The immediate future seemed pretty simple. If I kept moving, I would live. If I stopped? Maybe not. Probably not, even.

I didn't want to look too far ahead, didn't want to take anything for granted, but maybe if I got warmed up some, I'd try to make it to Doyle's and get a fire going. It was the only way forward I could think of. I didn't think that surviving the night was a true sign from God, but it meant something to me. I knew that I wanted to live. Even if I'd done wrong, even if I wasn't right in the head, I wanted to live a little longer, to breathe and think and stretch out my legs.

It occurred to me that I needed to stay hydrated, something that had slipped my mind in the cold. Drinking a cold glass of water is the last thing on your mind when you're shivering like this.

I strode to the bucket in the backroom, but I found a layer of ice atop it. I tapped at it, hoping to find that papery coat of frozen water that would clear out of the way without trouble like skin on top of soup or pudding, but no. It was thick. Solid. Not frozen through, but sturdy enough that I would need something hard and heavy to break it.

I abandoned the frozen bucket for the moment and did a couple more laps from the kitchen to the front door and back, keeping those muscles churning, the blood pumping. Deep breaths entered through my nostrils and inflated my chest, the shivers still coming on in pulses to try to shake the air out of me.

I pictured tools I could use, my brain a little slow to come up with options. I imagined a steak knife stabbing at the ice, but I knew that wasn't what I wanted, so I paused the movie in my head. The tool changed to an ice pick, the movie resuming, the pick jackhammering away, white shavings flying around. Then it switched mid-swing to a hammer pounding on the surface, the ice shattering after a couple of swings so crooked lines ran off an open hole in the middle of the bucket. Finally, my mind turned the hammer around, using the claw side as a nice compromise between the two approaches, offering a balance of piercing and bludgeoning at the same time.

Good. That would do.

I moved to the closet in the hall and knelt to rifle through the toolbox inside. The hammer was near the top of the pile, tucked under a few crisscrossing screwdrivers. My fingers found the handle and plucked it from the heap.

The ice caved in on the second hit, the hammer cracking through and plunging into the water with a sound reminiscent of the toilet. I ladled out a glass of water, trying to clear toilet thoughts from my head as I drank half of it and scooped out a refill.

I walked on, sipping at the drink as I did my rounds, forcing down mouthful after mouthful of the icy cold beverage. The shivers still rattled my sternum, still made my jaw quiver like I was about to burst into tears, but the sting had died down in my hands and feet. I thought I must be getting warmer.

Fiona

Beckley, West Virginia
151 days after

It was strange the way that primal desire to live, that human will to survive, overpowered all of the other feelings. I was feeling down after what happened with Doyle, and rightfully so, I supposed. Still, I didn't quite lie down and die. I hung in there, and that lust for life crept back up, snaked its way into my heart to make it bump again, to keep me moving, keep my feet shuffling over the floor, keep my body heat from getting sucked out into the cold.

I didn't know where I'd go. I didn't know what I'd do. But I was still here.

When I first heard the rumble of the engine outside, I thought it was in my head. I still paced the floor, some modicum of warmth finding its way into my limbs as I ambled around, the numbed out feelings giving way to pins and needles in the palms of my hands. I remembered having that paranoid sensation when the dawn first inched over the horizon, thinking that I must be hallucinating the light, and I remembered that I'd been wrong. Maybe I was wrong again.

I stopped and listened, that car's growl growing closer. I walked toward the front door, my feet now awkward as the rhythm of my gait changed. One hand unlatched the deadbolt, and the other twisted the doorknob and pulled it open.

The daylight streamed everywhere, intense in both brightness and the clarity of detail it revealed. Every blade of grass stood distinct from the rest. Every nick and flaw in the grain of the wood along the deck presented itself, like scars on a chin giving it character. After so long in the relative shade behind those frosted windows, these things took my breath away.

I stumbled forward a couple of paces, my feet pounding the wood planks, my eyes squinted down to slits even with a hand cupped around my brow for a little shade. The car sounded closer than I had anticipated, perhaps just a block or two off.

I didn't think. I moved toward it, feet thumping down the steps and crunching over the frozen grass. I blinked a few times, trying to coax my eyes into adjusting to the light out here, but it was hard to say if it helped at all.

When I got to the street, it occurred to me for the first time that I had no idea what I was getting myself into. I stopped. These could be killers. Rapists. Maybe even cannibals for all I knew. Who knew what people had resorted to out there? Doyle and I had come upon more than a few bodies we were quite sure had met violent ends, though the levels of decay often made it hard to say for sure what had happened. Slashed throats. Holes consistent with gunshot wounds. Deep purple strangle lines running rings around necks.

Once more I had a choice. I could choose the path of fear. I could turn back, stay safe but stay alone. Or I could choose the path of faith. I could walk into this danger, risking everything, putting all of my trust in whoever was driving out this way in a car.

I thought on it for a moment, the car engine shifting gears so the sound of the engine changed pitch. A little breeze blew into my face and the hair sticking out of my hat twitched in the wind.

I stepped forward.

Fiona

Gravity kicked in as I accelerated down the hill, my footsteps gone choppy and wild. More than jogging, I fell and caught myself over and over, one lunging step at a time. I barely even watched my feet, though, hardly saw the ground at all.

My gaze remained locked to the distance, fixed to the car I could just make out way down there. Light glinted on a sheet of glass, but it was hard to tell if it was the front or rear windshield. Was it coming toward me or moving away? I didn't know, so I ran.

I sloped down the mouth of a driveway and transitioned from the concrete of the sidewalk to the asphalt of the street. My speed built and built. It felt like if I stuck my arms out to my sides, I would take flight, curling up into the air into an arc to swoop down onto the car, pouncing on the roof like a cat, maybe with one leg splayed out to the side in some Spiderman-esque position.

Air rushed in and out of my lungs, cold and dry. I felt it in my nostrils, in my throat. And that little shake still persisted in my torso, muscles still convulsing, but it was different now. Adrenaline had morphed it into an electric throb, a trembling tingle that stayed constant instead of the rhythmic rattle from the cold.

The hill bottomed out into flat ground, and I kept going.

The run evened itself out, my gait going smooth, controlled, my knees and ankles no longer getting jammed with every step. My cheeks juddered with the bob of my footsteps, that pink flesh inside my mouth sliding up and down against my teeth, and I realized that my mouth had dropped open to keep up with my lungs.

The cold hugged around me, open air that stretched out in all directions. All of me felt exposed, uncovered, like that burning spot on the tip of my nose where the skin got peeled off.

The car looked like a dark SUV. Maybe black or navy blue. Possibly even purple. I squinted, my eyelids squeezing together so that my eyelashes filled my field of vision. I concentrated to look through them, letting them blur into the foreground. The vehicle's grill sharpened into focus first, and then the headlights formed alongside each side of it, and I knew it was headed my way.

People. Real live people sitting behind the glare on the windshield just ahead. I almost vomited from the sheer stimulation of it.

I lifted my arms up over my head and waved them, wrists crossing over each other and separating. I didn't realize I was yelling until my voice cracked. I sounded dry, harsh, more like a bird's warning cry than a call out for help, I thought. I knew it was doubtful anyone could hear me from this distance, especially with the windows up, but I yelled anyway.

I blinked a few times, watched everything go from bright to dark and back. My heart sped up and my eyes went wide. I almost panicked when the car disappeared for even a second behind the flesh of my eyelids, like that was a real risk, the sedan might just vanish into a puff of smoke, or roll away from me if I looked away at all. It was almost like the most superstitious part of my brain believed that my eyeballs held some sway over the car's movements or even its existence altogether.

All things drifted into slow motion when the SUV got within a block of me. I could see the vehicle better now, an older model Jeep Grand Cherokee from what I could make out, at least 15 or 20 years old. Black as I'd first thought. The light rippled on the hood and windshield, the reflections morphing into new shapes as the shiny surfaces slid toward me.

I knew this was it. My prospects for living or dying might well be settled in these next few minutes, as though my life, my fate would rest on a single roll of the dice. Were the people sitting behind the glare on the windshield kind or hostile? Let's see what the dice have to say.

The car slowed as it drew near. I could make out silhouettes, moving shapes behind the glass, but not faces. It looked to be two people, but with the glare obscuring my view, I couldn't be certain.

I dropped to my knees and left my hands above my head, no longer waving. I didn't consciously consider it at the time, but I guess it was an act of submission. I didn't want to seem a threat in any way, so I threw myself at the mercy of these strangers entirely, making it clear that they would choose my destiny for good or ill.

My chest heaved, and I sucked in air, ragged breaths scraping at my dried out throat. My heart still hammered against the horizontal bars of my ribcage, not yet willing to slow back down.

The Jeep inched toward me, only about fifteen feet out now, creeping forward so slowly that I could make out the tread on the tires in full detail. Every groove. Every divot. And then the wheels stopped. I could sense the faintest jerk in the vehicle as the driver shifted it into park.

I closed my eyes, focused all of my attention onto the sound of the SUV's engine, the feeling of the cold blacktop seeping into my knees serving as the lone distraction. The pitch shifted a half a step higher now that the car idled in park.

When I opened my eyes, the driver's side door was opened a wedge. A foot stepped through below the door, and then a face bobbed into the opening above it. A smiling face, his eyes seeking mine and locking onto them.

I gasped.

For I knew the silver-haired man who stood before me, the laugh lines around the eyes, the strong jaw. It was the preacher, the one from TV. Ray Dalton. And I knew in my heart that this was no coincidence. No random chance had brought us together. It was the sign from God I had been waiting for.

Fiona

Beckley, West Virginia
151 days after

Dalton and his friend Lorraine wait in the Grand Cherokee
outside while I gather up the last of my things. From here,
we'll head to the little camp they've set up. They're building a
group, a community, in Western Maryland. 49 strong and
growing. They went on a road trip to look for people who
needed help as soon as the snow cleared, recruiting trips they
call them. And because of the route they took today, I will
become number 50.

It seems entirely random, but I know it's not. It's the
group I've dreamed of all along. I won't even be alone on
Christmas.

I burst into tears as Dalton explained these things to me,
childlike sobs pouring out of me. I wanted to tell them about
what happened with Doyle, about the dreams and the
strychnine, about how everything went bad while we were
here on our own, but Lorraine stopped me.

"You can't look back. You have to let go. We all did things
to survive. All of us. We all crossed lines we didn't think we'd
cross, but this is a fresh start for everyone. A new society. A
new harmony, a new order that we will create together, piece
by piece. The world as it existed before is gone, and
everything that happened before is erased. It's a new
beginning for each of us."

She rubbed the back of my hand while she talked, and I let the words of Doyle's story die in my throat. The tears still poured out for a while yet, but I stayed quiet.

Now my things are packed up, the last load just about to go out to the trunk of the SUV. I wish I could go out back and bury Doyle, but there's no way. Like Lorraine said, I can't look back. I have to let go.

This notebook is pretty well full, and I suppose that makes more than one reason to leave it behind.

Here's to a fresh start.

Decker

South of Pittsburgh, Pennsylvania
159 days after

It's Christmas. My first Christmas since everyone died, and I am sick. Really sick. I don't think I'm going to make it.

Christmas-pocalypse. Shit. I think I had something better than that. Can't remember.

My brain feels swollen in my head, so much pressure in my skull like someone shook up a two liter of Dr. Pepper in there, and I've vomited everything I have eaten for the past six days. I keep water down, it seems. Everything else comes roaring back up to paint an abstract picture.

I lie here in my bed and look out the window at the snow everywhere, my blanket draped across my legs. I sleep and wake and the day goes bright and dark out there, the days go by, the time dries out and blows away.

Every so often I rise on shaky legs, stumbling through the house to piss and get another pitcher of water, throw my bucket of vomit away. Wood floors creak underfoot, and I lurch and sway like a ship navigating a stormy sea.

I didn't have the energy to keep the fire going, so the cold crept into the house, into my room little by little. There were times I could see my breath even lying in bed.

I don't know what has inspired me to write or where I'm even finding the energy to do it, the clarity to do it. But the fog has cleared some, and I think I wanted to say that I'm sorry. That I was wrong, and that I regret some of the things I've done. If there is a God, he will know which ones I mean. I lost it for a while there, embraced madness as a way to survive, embraced that animal part of me, and it was wrong. That's not who I am, or at least, it's not who I was before all of this.

Winter is here. The end of things. Many creatures don't survive it, so at least I'm not alone in that sense. Our dirt nap will be like a big sleepover.

I have wondered off and on if the illness I have is the plague. I'm not sure, really. At first I thought maybe I ate something that was off. Some damaged can full of strange bacteria. I haven't vomited blood or anything like that, but neither did my mom. We're not bleeders. In any case, I think I'm all done.

This isn't a suicide letter, but it's not far off.

Weird memories keep coming upon me as vivid as can be. I remember sitting with my mom in our apartment when I was a kid, the window unit blasting, and the room cold enough to make my glass of Sprite sweat. It was late. Dark. I folded out the couch in the living room, where I sometimes slept in the summer for fun, like camping, almost, and I sat there on that thin mattress and flipped through the channels, watching a bunch of music videos that made no sense to me. I remember the acid and sweet of the Sprite on my tongue, the chill of the air conditioner eventually leading me to retract my arms through my sleeves to hug against my torso inside of my shirt.

I remember finding a Playboy at my Dad's house when I was really young, looking at the photos of naked women, aroused yet perplexed, not quite sure how their genitalia worked.

Is this what happens when you're dying? Shards of your life come back to you one by one, exactly as they felt? Movies play in your head, fragments of your time relived?

I plead with myself, with my imagination, to find a way to come to grips with death before it arrives, to find a way to accept that inevitable fate. But how? What am I supposed to do with that information if and when I'm able to truly process it? That's the paradox that runs all through life, I guess, at least for me.

I've perpetually found myself convinced that I can't live a life that makes sense without understanding my imminent death and making a real effort to incorporate the idea of mortality into my worldview. I feel like if I don't connect with that, my life gets lost in a series of fast food moments – my actions and relationships and thoughts veer toward easy answers, perpetual consumption, comfort and convenience valued above all else with no sense of meaning underneath. I forget to hold onto the passion of being alive, falling into taking it for granted, into that grind of production and consumption that becomes daily life. Everything becomes easy, neat, packaged, tidy, thoughtless. Every day becomes the same thing, the same color and shape and taste, like life itself should come with fries if you want them.

And yet when I attempt to grapple with mortality, attempt to incorporate it into my worldview, I find no actionable way forward with that nugget of information. What am I supposed to do with it? What path to redemption presents itself when one eschews comfort and a thoughtless sense of immortality in favor of a realistic view? I can't find it. Even now, on what seems to be my deathbed, I can't find it. When I get glimpses of death, of the real thing, life only seems more pointless.

I remember back in the empty apartment building, I tried to throw that idea of worrying about mortality away, tried to throw the idea of meaning itself away. I chose to live as an animal, live in the moment and take what I wanted. In some ways, I still think that approach makes the most sense, which terrifies me. I don't want to believe it, but I kind of do.

Argh. I need to fill my water bucket, stumbling out into the cold, crunching out to pump that well handle. It adds up to quite an exertion, which I'm sure will drain the rest of my energy and leave me dizzy and panting. We'll see, though. Here goes.

Indeed. I'm tired now, too cold and tired to go on, so I think I will set this aside. I don't want to look back on these words, or I'll wonder why I wrote them down at all. Funny how this spiral of thoughts never stops spinning, isn't it? The words come cascading out like a waterfall, and they won't stop until my body goes cold and rigid, until my consciousness divorces itself from my body and shuffles off to some other place.

Or maybe nowhere.

THE SCATTERED AND THE DEAD

For information on the next installment of The Scattered and the Dead, please visit http://LTVargus.com

SPREAD THE WORD

Thank you for reading! We'd be very grateful if you could take a few minutes to review it on Amazon.com.

How grateful? Eternally. Even when we are old and dead and have turned into ghosts, we will be thinking fondly of you and your kind words. The most powerful way to bring our books to the attention of other people is through the honest reviews from readers like you.

COME PARTY WITH US

We're loners. Rebels. But much to our surprise, the most kickass part of writing has been connecting with our readers. From time to time, we send out newsletters with giveaways, special offers, and juicy details on new releases.

Sign up for our mailing list at:
http://ltvargus.com/mailing-list/

ABOUT THE AUTHORS

Tim McBain writes because life is short, and he wants to make something awesome before he dies. Additionally, he likes to move it, move it.

You can connect with Tim on Twitter at @realtimmcbain or via email at tim@timmcbain.com.

L.T. Vargus grew up in Hell, Michigan, which is a lot smaller, quieter, and less fiery than one might imagine. When not click-clacking away at the keyboard, she can be found sewing, fantasizing about food, and rotting her brain in front of the TV.

If you want to wax poetic about pizza or cats, you can contact L.T. (the L is for Lex) at ltvargus9@gmail.com or on Twitter @ltvargus.

TimMcBain.com

LTVargus.com